"GO TO HIM, CHILD," THE COMTESSE ORDERED KINDLY.

Obediently, Georgianna did as she was told, trembling a little as the Marquis' hooded eyes raked her face.

"So . . ." His lip curled slightly. "Can this really be the same girl I found standing in a cart-track not three weeks ago?" He turned to his aunt. "You are to be congratulated."

Under his hands Georgianna shivered, as much at the tone of his words as at the touch of his fingers on her skin. She sensed he was under some great strain, and, unknowingly, provided the final straw.

"My gown is very pretty," she said, "a little like the one your Mama is wearing in her portrait."

Three pairs of eyes rested on the portrait, but when Georgianna turned to look at her guardian, she almost fell back in alarm at the fury and rage upon his face.

"I'm glad you fancy there is some similarity," he said, "for it won't be long before you find yourself sharing the same fate. She wasn't laughing the last time I saw her, neither was she looking so pretty. That portrait was painted when she was seventeen, just before her marriage to my father. Only a year younger than you. She died before she was thirty."

Without another word the Marquis was gone, only the echo of the slammed door left to remind them he had ever been present.

Novels by Caroline Courtney

Duchess in Disguise
A Wager For Love
Love Unmasked
Guardian of The Heart
Dangerous Engagement
Fortunes of Love

Published by
WARNER BOOKS

CAROLINE COURTNEY

Guardian of the Heart

WARNER BOOKS

A Warner Communications Company

Chapter 1

The exterior of Rossington House presented an imposing façade to the world. Its sheer size dominated Rossington Square, dwarfing its neighbors. Inside, the entrance hall was large, cold, and lofty, perfectly square with three doors opening down each side of it, and an extremely fine marble staircase rising gracefully to branch out into two galleries. Perhaps it was the profusion of marble that gave the house its cold air—not content with having his staircase carved from it, the Third Marquis had also had it laid upon his floor, in a formal design of black and white. The effect was completed with an army of busts, standing guard outside each door, staring blindly from their plinths at those bold enough to seek entrance.

Today the house seemed to wear an even chillier aspect than usual. Maybe it was because it had been closed up for so many months, or perhaps it was the fault of the gusting April wind. In any case, the gentleman descending the marble staircase quite obviously was not disposed to linger in the hallway long enough

5

to discover. He crossed the expanse of black-and-white floor in a manner that was at once languid and yet held a hint of lean, coiled strength, somewhat at variance with his modish appearance. A coat of rich blue velvet fell open to reveal a waistcoat of cream brocade, lavishly embroidered in blue and gold, heavy falls of lace embracing both the gentleman's neck and wrists. The cream satin small-clothes fitted to a nicety; silk stockings clocked with blue and cream, displaying well-muscled legs.

His footsteps rang coldly across the stone. Two flunkeys in their blue-and-gold livery sprang to attention; the double doors opened on smoothly oiled hinges, and the gentleman stepped into the room.

The library of Rossington House was no different from any of the other rooms. It was overly large, decorated in the exuberant Rococo fashion of some twenty years past, its molded ceiling flaunting paintings after the fashion of Le Brun; the God of War, Mars, dark and menacing descending from the clouds, surrounded by attendant nymphs and cherubs.

The gentleman's cool gray eyes rested thoughtfully upon the book shelves, their wood gleaming softly, the muted reds, blues, and greens of the leatherbound books bringing a touch of warmth to the room. The air was redolent with the smell of leather and parchment, the enormous fire burning in the grate throwing out tongues of flame, flickering and reflecting upon mirror and glass, the faint draught from the door setting the chandelier shattering into a thousand dancing points of light.

Despite the fire, the luxurious thickness of the Aubusson carpet, and the heavy velvet drapes, the room was still cold, with the same chill that pervaded the entire house; austere and repelling; giving off to the more sensitive an aura of bitterness, of hopes that had been slowly and silently starved and suffocated, of love that had never been allowed to grow, of people as icily distant as the house itself.

However, it was apparent that the gentleman was not one of these sensitive souls, for he crossed to a small mahogany table and poured himself a generous measure of claret, the rich, warm liquid bringing the crystal to life, glowing in the firelight, catching and refracting a thousand times the cold gleam of the diamonds gracing the long, elegant fingers as he lifted the glass to his lips.

Seen in profile, the gentleman's features had something of a predatory look about them, proud and remote, vaguely reminiscent of a bird of prey, at once both beautiful and cruel, the skin drawn tight over the bones of his face; a face without a trace of gentleness or warmth and yet a face that drew the eye again and again. Indeed, impressive though Rossington House was with its marble, its *hauteur*, its air of standing out from the crowd, it was certainly in no way as impressive as its new owner, Justin Sebastion Bertrand Ormsby, Comte de Saint-Vire and more recently, Fifth Marquis of Rossington, a gentleman who like his home announced quite clearly to the world: "This far and no farther."

He drank the claret apparently lost in

thoughts, which to judge from his expression were far from pleasant, although there were those who would have said that it was his normal expression, and that Justin Saint-Vire never looked out upon the world with anything other than sardonic contempt. As he drank he read once again the document lying on the small table: "The Last Will and Testament of Sir John Lawley."

And it was this, the will of a gentleman completely unknown to him, that had brought him back to England and Rossington House.

His mouth twisted in bitterness. It had taken a complete stranger to make him break a vow he had made over ten years ago. A stranger and a child. He threw back his head and laughed, a harsh, mirthless sound, the last dying rays of the thin April sunshine turning his dark hair to the blue-black gleam of a raven's wing, throwing into relief the aquiline features, revealing unmercifully the skepticism that was so much a part of the man and that sat so easily upon his broad shoulders.

He glanced at the clock. Soon his man of business should be with him, and hopefully he would learn exactly why a complete stranger should have seen fit to make him the guardian of his only child. A smile of painful bitterness touched his mouth. It wasn't for nothing that he was known as the most notorious rake ever to grace the court of Versailles, and he had few illusions as to Society's reaction to the news that he was now the legal guardian of someone else's offspring. Doubtless before too long they would be saying the child was his by-blow. His whole face tightened and the man entering the room saw the look and wondered at it.

He cleared his throat a little nervously, searching the Marquis's arrogant features, trying to judge his mood.

"Ah, Jervington. So, how does the matter of Sir John's will progress? Doubtless you have, in your inestimable fashion, solved our little dilemma?" Was there a faint challenge in the cool eyes, a touch of mockery in the disinterested voice? The lawyer could not tell. He only knew that the Marquis, returned from Paris only a few days ago, glittering and awe-inspiring in his silks and satins, with the formidable air of sophistication gained in the most hedonistic court in all Europe, made him feel more aware of his own deficiencies than any other person he had known.

A handful of days, that was all it had taken, and already London was awash with rumors, most of which pointed to the fact that the new Marquis, far from being made in the same mold as his august forebears, was little better than a libertine and a womanizer. Master Jervington, never one to make a hasty judgment, merely reflected that it was a great pity that such a young and handsome countenance should be so deeply marred by cynicism and boredom.

As the lawyer made no comment, apart from a rather despairing glance, the Marquis was left to form his own conclusions.

"Well, Jervington, am I to take it then that

you have not been able to deal with the matter?"

This was the moment the lawyer had been dreading.

"The will is quite irrefutable," he offered at last. "There can be no doubt."

The room seemed to grow quiet and dark, even the fire ceasing its pleasant crackling. He glanced once at the Marquis, and then when he saw his quite openly bitter expression he wished he had not.

"I see. Well, perhaps then you can explain to me the nature of Sir John's little jest. He was, I take it, quite out of his mind?"

On this point at least the lawyer could reassure him.

"I do not believe the late Sir John ever intended you to become the guardian of his child."

Resolutely he ignored the mocking expression.

"I have discovered that Sir John and your late father . . ."

He stumbled a little over the words, damning the Fate that had brought him to this pass. The Marquis's quarrel with his parent had been intense and bitter, and had resulted in the boy leaving England and taking up residence in the enormous Paris hotel bequeathed to him as part of his mother's estate. Just what the quarrel was about no one knew. Some said it was over the boy's wild behavior, others said it was due to the father's ill treatment of his wife. Some murmured of a secret duel fought between father and son, but whatever the truth, it was kept hidden. All that was known was that the boy had left, vowing never to set foot in England, and more particularly, Rossington House, ever again. The Marquis's father was dead now. It had happened quite quickly, a stroke some two years ago, leaving only the boy's grandfather, the Fourth Marquis of Rossington, his remaining relative in England.

"Yes," prodded the Marquis smoothly, "you have discovered precisely what about Sir John and my late unlamented parent, Jervington?"

This was no time for finesse. The lawyer plunged on.

"I believe that Sir John intended your father to be the child's guardian."

The words fell into a small pool of silence. There was a marked degree of sarcasm in the drawling voice when the Marquis eventually replied.

"Indeed, am I to understand then that the late Sir John was gifted with a foresight denied lesser mortals?"

Flustered the lawyer gasped, "Foresight?"

The Marquis sighed gently. "Yes, Jervington, foresight. In designating my father the Fifth Marquis of Rossington. A trifle precipitate to say the least, wouldn't you agree, especially in view of the fact that when the will was drawn up, my grandfather, the Fourth Marquis, was still very much alive?"

Jervington dabbed frantically at his forehead with a large handkerchief, mentally cursing the folly of the late Sir John, struggling manfully to provide an explanation for the totally ridiculous circumstances the Marquis now found himself in.

There was an intense, brooding look on the younger man's face that he found distinctly unnerving, and he could not help pitying the child who would shortly find himself under the Marquis's care. He banished the thought as disloyal, but still it would keep returning. The Marquis was not the person to have the upbringing of a young child. Almost as though he read his thoughts the Marquis prompted, "You were saying, Jervington, the will, and my ward." Again his face twisted in that hauntingly bitter smile.

"The will. Yes, a most regrettable error. Had I known what your father and Sir John had in mind." He shrugged depreciatingly. "In the natural course of events one night, I suppose, have expected your father to inherit. That is . . ." His voice faltered into a morass of half-finished sentences, as he sought vainly to extricate himself. Heroically he tried again, resolutely ignoring the steely glint with which he was being regarded. "Apparently the will was drawn up shortly after Sir John married. He and your father were old friends, they were at Eton together and in the same regiment for a time, I believe."

"Friends were they?" mused the Marquis, "and so Sir John trusts his only child to my father's care, even though they could not have met for years. What is the boy's name again? Georgy, I believe. No doubt named after our revered monarch. Such are the workings of fate, Jervington, that the boy now comes into my care."

The lawyer had been on the point of explaining that the hurriedly drawn-up will had been lodged with Sir John's man of business and left to gather dust until his recent demise. However, he asked unsteadily, "Your care? But surely you will not want to be burdened with the child?"

The Marquis answered, "You think not? What had you in mind then, Jervington? The child has relatives perhaps?"

The lawyer, allowing himself to relax a little, shook his head. "No, there is no one, no one at all."

In his eagerness he missed the faintly pleased glint in the depths of the gray eyes.

"But if I might venture to suggest, perhaps a good school, a respectable couple who might be prepared to take charge of the boy until he is grown?"

One winged eyebrow rose slightly. "You don't think that might be construed as a little cold-blooded then, Jervington? I mean, with the child's father scarcely cold in his grave, you don't feel that perhaps I ought to take an interest in the brat myself?" Since this was precisely what the lawyer did not feel, he hastened to reassure the Marquis.

It would be unthinkable for the Marquis to saddle himself with the responsibility of the boy, a responsibility that was only his by virtue of a mistake in the first place. No, no, let him be installed at a good school, or placed with some worthy family for a few months.

The Marquis eyed him in sardonic amusement.

"It occurs to me, Jervington, that you are

attempting to provide me with a loophole. I wonder why. For my benefit or for the child's? However, I'm sure I am right in thinking that the will explicitly states that I should be the sole guardian of this young person?"

Hastily the lawyer denied any such intention.

"You cannot possibly want to be burdened with him."

"You think not? I assure you, Jervington, you are quite wrong." Something in the purred words and the look that accompanied them made the lawyer's heart sink. He had been right to be uneasy. Bravely he asked, "But why?"

"Because it is my will, Jervington. Can you think of a better reason?" Appalled, the lawyer fell back. There was nothing he could do. The child was the Marquis's ward. He looked into the implacable face and shivered, but it was too late to protest, already he was being ushered to the door. "Rossington, I beg you, think again," he implored, but it was no use.

"Good day, Jervington."

The double doors closed in his face, leaving him standing foolishly in the hallway.

Left alone, the Marquis poured another glass of claret, his expression somber, lightening a little as he recollected the lawyer's pathetic attempts to get him to give up the child.

The Marquis laughed soundlessly. How strange the workings of Fate, giving into his hands the method of wreaking vengeance upon his father. It mattered little to him that this father was now beyond all human revenge; it could still be accomplished, with this child, the offspring of his father's best friend. Anger and hatred welled up inside him. The long, fine fingers crushed the glass, uncaring that the claret was dripping onto the carpet like blood, or that the splinters of glass were being ground into the palm of his hand. He was aware of nothing but the desire to wreak vengeance against his father, for all that he had made him suffer by in turn. . . . He paused for a moment, lifting his head to stare blindly through the window. In turn what? Treating this child as his father had treated him, giving him everything that money could buy, but no affection, no love. He smiled again, faintly, cruelly. Why not? The child should have everything he could give him; everything but the one thing he would need most. This boy who had probably been well loved by his father, a man who in turn his own father had loved. Never once did it strike him that to do so might be to harm the child, that to wreak such revenge on the innocent was an appalling crime; he had long since immured himself against the feelings of others. The child was but a pawn in the game of life. He unclenched his hand, surprised to see that it was bleeding where the tiny slivers of glass had lacerated the skin.

He glanced upward at the familiar portrait of his father, cold, distant, a man without human feelings or failings, and then he thought of his lovely French mother, warm, laughing, hauntingly beautiful. At least she had been until his father had slowly crushed the laughter and warmth from her, ignoring her presence in his house, making it all too plain that for him the marriage was merely a matter of convenience. Again the bitter smile appeared. What convenience there had been had all been on his father's side. It was his mother who had possessed the fortune; his mother who could have married the highest in the land in France and yet who had wed his father, and then been left to wilt, like the soft-scented mimosa of the South, left to die in the cold, harsh winds of the North.

She died while he had been at Eton, not dramatically, but slowly slipping away quietly, but she had had her revenge. All that she possessed, all those lands and riches that should have been her husband's were now her son's.

He recalled his own tears at her death, and his father's harshness. Rossingtons did not cry, and the cost of his tears were three long days in a cold room with bread and milk. Still it had taught him a lesson; he had never cried since. He had been nine then. In another man reflections might have served to soften his purpose, but in the Comte de Saint-Vire they merely hardened it. The boy and his feelings were immaterial; all that mattered was that he was the son of his father's best friend.

There had never been any lack of female companionship in his life, as his reputation could testify, but it was not the number of his amours that shocked the Ton, but rather the manner in which they were conducted. The callous indifference with which his mistresses were treated once they had served their purpose, their place in his life clearly and firmly delineated. But if they found his passion as icily cold as the depths of his gray eyes, it certainly did not seem to deter them. He would watch in cynical disinterest while they strived to bring warmth and admiration to his eyes, and love to his desire.

He smiled a little sardonically as he reflected upon his last mistress. She was extremely beautiful and passionate, but there was a tendency to be somewhat overemotional, and worse still, possessive. The Marquis had a marked dislike for possessive women.

His mouth curled faintly. Women are fools. They sought to deceive with their warm glances and coaxing ways, using all their charms to beguile what they fondly thought of as a helpless male, but the Marquis was not so easily enchanted. He well knew what could lurk under a pretty face and an innocent manner. Many ladies who had thought to the contrary and had attempted to cajole or coax from him some favor or other had found that the gently ironic manner could turn all too swiftly into implacable determination. They were to find themselves swiftly disabused of the notion that they had the power to sway the gentleman from his chosen course. And worse still, following hard upon the heels of such scenes, they had found themselves coldly and quickly displaced in the Marquis's affections, or at least what passed for them, for one thing was more than obvious: He had never entertained the slightest degree of love for a single one of the many women who had thus far shared his bed.

Saint-Vire, it was agreed, was a law unto himself and no respector of the creeds that bound other, and possibly lesser, men.

Whatever his private plans for the future of his ward might have been, nothing showed in his demeanor when the new Marquis sauntered into White's later that evening.

He was barely over the threshold when he was accosted by a cheerful cry.

"Saint-Vire, By all that's Holy. I didn't know you were in London. Heard about your grandfather's death, of course."

As though realizing he was on uneasy ground, the young gentleman broke off.

"Versailles palling on you, is it? Lord knows, I don't know how you can stand it. Only went there once, and that was enough."

"There are compensations, Peter," responded the Marquis dryly.

"Aye, so I hear," returned Sir Peter Forester bluntly.

"Called round at Mountmont's the other day. His cousin is the British Ambassador you must know, and he was all ahum with your doings."

"Indeed," came the careless reply, "he must have remarkably little to do if he needs to pass the time in idle gossip."

Far from dampening his spirits this merely had the effect of drawing a reluctant grin from the younger man.

"I hear there's a friend of yours recently arrived in London, Saint-Vire. From France," he added importantly.

"Really."

It was obvious the Marquis was not to be drawn.

"Aye, she was at the Devonshire's ball. Asked most particularly after you."

"She?" inquired the Marquis delicately.

"The Comtesse de Liveaurac."

All at once the Marquis's face darkened.

"I trust the lady has not come to England specifically to see me?"

Sir Peter looked increasingly uncomfortable.

"She is not a friend then?"

The Marquis flicked open his snuff box, took a minute pinch, and then closed it firmly.

"A friend," he mused. "That depends, Peter, on how one defines friendship. You are a friend. The lady comes into a different category altogether. I do not count my mistresses as friends."

Sir Peter turned away, a little discomposed. This was Saint-Vire at his worst. As though he sensed the young man's discomfort he relented a little.

"Forgive me, Peter, a hand of piquet perhaps?"

"What, and lose what little money I have left?"

Nevertheless he acquiesced and allowed himself to be led to the tables.

The Marquis was in his dressing room, being divested of his riding dress with the able assistance of his valet when a visitor swept past the bemused footman and into the hall. She did not pause by the marble busts, nor did she spare a glance for the fine staircase as her heels tapped angrily across the floor. In a cloud of heavy perfume and a barrage of extremely voluble French, she addressed herself to the butler, breaking off in exasperation as she saw his total lack of comprehension. She raised her thin-penciled eyebrows heavenward.

"Tiens! You English. Barbarians! Your master, Saint-Vire." She clicked her fingers, "Rossington. You may tell him that I am here. *Depechez,"* she commanded. *"Vite!"*

The Rossington household were not used to dealing with the sudden eruption of beautiful and extremely colorful women demanding to see their master. However, Johnson, rose nobly to the occasion, frowning darkly at the goggling footmen and showing the visitor into the well-appointed, though cheerless, withdrawing room.

This feat having been accomplished he instructed a wide-eyed footman to appraise the Marquis of the fact that there was someone waiting to see him.

The Marquis regarded the footman calmly, and then instructed him to tell the lady that he would be with her shortly.

The fall of lace at his throat was adjusted to his liking, the fine silk stockings drawn over the well-formed legs; the rose satin smoothed reverendly over the broad shoulders. The addition of a diamond here and there, a small pin nestling in the foaming white lace, the thick dark hair brushed back and constrained in a neat riband. The Marquis rose, coldly dismissing the hovering valet, and picked up his snuff box. He paused for a moment, shaking out the lace ruffles at his cuffs, and with his habitual mask of cynical amusement, slowly descended the stairs.

He paused for a moment in the hall to allow the slouching flunkey to collect himself, giving him a look that made that young man very much aware of his deficiencies, before motioning to him to throw open the doors, to allow him to saunter into the room.

The lady was standing looking out onto the square, one small foot tapping impatiently. She swung round at his entrance, gliding toward him with a provocative feline grace. If she had looked for surprise, she found none. He merely stepped forward, fobbing off her attempt to embrace him by the simple expedient of taking both her hands in his, glancing at her in cool arrogance.

"*Ma chere* Louise. What brings you to London?"

Louise de Liveaurac hesitated for a moment, and then with her customary poise, affected a small pout, at the same time removing a very charming Villager hat to reveal glossy sable ringlets, an excellent foil for her lilac gown.

"Justin, *mon amour*." She had a low, husky voice, which she used to good effect, only the slight hardening of her eyes betraying her chagrin at this less-than-warm welcome. Producing a miniscule scrap of lace she dabbed effectively at her violet eyes.

"Justin, I implore you."

Firmly disengaging himself, the Marquis eyed her coldly.

"What brings you to London, Louise?"

Her eyes flashed at his tone. He knew well enough what brought her. "You, of course, Justin, what else?" Instantly she realised she had gone too far. The gray eyes rested thoughtfully on her.

"How very flattering, Louise, but what could you possibly want with me now?"

Dieu, he could ask her that? Had he no feelings at all? He must know how she felt about him. She had made it plain enough in all conscience.

She chose to ignore his question, adopting instead a manner at once both pleading and chagrined.

"Lud, Justin, first you keep me waiting like some common serving wench and then when you do appear you are so cold and disapproving."

Another pout accompanied the words. "I swear it is this vile English weather that affects you so. You were not like this in Paris." She moistened her lips slightly. "And to leave without even telling me."

"Forgive me, my dear." His voice was a mockery of politeness. "But you see I did not consider my movements were really any of your concern." Beneath his careless scrutiny her face paled. He wasn't even going to make any pretense of being polite.

Her fur muff was tossed ruthlessly aside as she ran toward him, his name leaving her lips on a tormented cry.

"Justin."

Once again he held her off, this time without even the saving grace of gentleness.

"I neither know nor care what your purpose in seeking me out in this fashion is, Louise, but as far as I am concerned I have already said all I wish to say to you. We have already made our farewells, or have you forgotten?"

Faint color ran up under the lovely skin. Forgotten! How could she possibly forget that scene in her boudoir, or the callous words with which he had given her her *congé?* Since she had come to Paris as an impoverished young widow, Louise had had many lovers, but never one like Saint Vire. Even now she could not believe she had lost him. She bit her lip in vexation. Far better to have remained in Paris and prayed that he might return to her than to have chased after him in such a foolish fashion.

His contempt lashed her pride, but even worse was his obvious indifference. She was not used to having to plead for favors. Her longing showed quite unashamedly in her face as she murmured.

"*Tiens,* Justin, but you make it hard for me. You must know how much I have missed you. How I have wanted you." Her voice broke on the words. She was humbling herself as she had never done before, pleading with him, inviting his contempt, but she no longer cared.

"Justin," she begged.

It was a vain plea. Calmly the Marquis removed the clutching fingers, his action expressing his distaste more plainly than any words, and so physically slighting that she almost flinched beneath it.

23

"No scenes, my dear, I beg. They are so infinitely wearying, and besides, I had thought you understood."

"Understood?" Her voice faltered over the word, her eyes avoiding the merciless scrutiny of his, trying to convince herself that all was not lost.

"What am I to understand?"

Deep within her there was a momentary *frisson* of alarm. Surely he would relent now that she had let him see how much she cared for him. Never before had any man refused what she had offered, and never had she offered it so blatantly. She was far too lost to all sense of discretion to know that merely by showing her feelings so openly she was defeating her own object. She only knew a strange sinking feeling as she looked into the eyes she had seen cloudy with desire and the lips that had so often held her own captive.

Many had warned her about the Marquis, but she had ignored them, sure of her own power, sure that she would keep him when others had not. After all, was she not beautiful and young? She had smiled at those who had whispered in her ear that he never stayed long with one woman, growing bored and casting them aside, but now as she read the purpose in his eyes, panic filled her. She could not give him up. She would not. Incautiously she tried to plead afresh.

"Justin, please. In the name of all that we have shared. Surely you cannot have forgotten so soon?"

"My dear." The pitying words made her

lose the last of her control. She thought of her brother, Jules Clary, waiting in Paris and shivered.

Monsieur Clary had made good use of his sister's beauty. He would be none too pleased to learn she had allowed Saint-Vire to slip through her fingers. He had warned her not to be too sanguine. Another tremor shook her. There was something about her brother at times that frightened her.

"Justin, have you no pity?"

It was a pointless question, and she knew it from the cruel smile he gave her.

"Ah, so it's my pity you want, is it, Louise? I had thought it something else."

Before she could stop herself, she burst out: "But, Justin, I love you!"

A faintly bored expression crept over the Marquis's face. "Do you, my dear? Singularly foolish of you. I had thought we understood one another. A pleasant interlude, nothing more."

Her eyes darkened with pain. "Is that all I meant to you? A pleasant interlude?" She did not wait for an answer. "I tell you this now, Justin: One day you, too, will fall in love, and when you do I pray that she will hurt you as you have hurt me."

She got to her feet, her body trembling so much she could barely stand. She had never for one moment thought he would treat her like this. She would have to return to Paris alone. If only he would relent. She paused at the door but there was nothing but that cruel, mocking smile on his face. She had gambled and lost.

Once she had gone the Marquis stood by

the fire, his expression unreadable. Louise was a greater fool than he had imagined.

Love. A word for green girls; a word to cover a variety of less pleasant emotions, desire, need, passion, greed, but love itself . . .

He recalled the words of his mother's cousin, Claudine du Farnand. What was it she had said to him?

"Every man needed to fall deeply in love at least once in his lifetime, otherwise he was not truly a man."

True or not, it was something he had no intention of doing. Never would he abandon himself to an emotion that demanded the total abnegation of self, the submersion of one's control and will. It would be as foolish and as unnecessary as jumping off the roof of Rossington House.

Somehow the thought of love brought him back to the subject of his ward. He thought of what Versailles could do to a young and impressionable boy. Sir John Lawley had left no money, but he intended to be a generous guardian; the boy should have ample funds to indulge himself in anything that took his fancy. He dwelt without compunction on the faces of the pages at Versailles. Their eyes were old and world-weary, with a knowledge far beyond their years, and then he thought of his mother, her lovely shining beauty slowly destroyed, choked to death in the cold, hostile atmosphere of this house. His mind was made up. There could be no going back.

Chapter
2

Deep in the heart of the countryside, some thirty miles from London, another person was also spending a good deal of time in contemplation of the matter of the late Sir John's will. None other than his sole offspring, Georgy, or to give that young person her full title, for indeed "Georgy" was not as both the Marquis and his man of business had supposed a boy, but a girl— Miss Georgianna Lawley. Since she had first learned of her guardian's existence, he had become the main topic of conversation at the manor.

"I wonder what he will be like, this Marquis?" She now murmured reflectively, taking another bite of her apple and munching thoughtfully for a moment. "It seems strange that Papa should never have even mentioned him to me, don't you think Batesy? Especially if they were such good friends? And they must have been, mustn't they, otherwise Papa would not have made him my guardian?" There was a hint of uncertainty in her voice. "I wonder when it was all arranged? I can't remember Papa so much as setting a foot outside the village after Mama died. What do you think, Batesy?"

The woman thus addressed looked up briefly from her task, before applying herself with renewed vigor to rolling out her pastry.

"What do I think about what, Miss Georgie?"

A small dimple appeared in one damask cheek. Georgianna hunched forward, hugging her knees.

"You know full well what about, Batesy," she accused. "About my guardian, of course. The Marquis . . ." She hunted frantically on the table, pouncing triumphantly on a piece of paper. . . . "The Marquis of Rossington. Aren't you even the slightest bit curious? I mean it's very odd, isn't it?"

Mrs. Bates pursed her lips repressively.

"T'ain't for the likes of me to question the ways of the quality, miss. If your Papa thought it right to make this man your guardian, then right it must be. Still . . ." she paused for a second, eying the girl consideringly.

"If you are me, 'tis a good thing. T'ain't proper for a young lady like you to be left alone here without anyone to watch out for you. T'ain't right at all. If your poor mama were alive things would be different." She shook her head gravely.

"I don't say your Papa wasn't a good man in his way, but . . ."

"But he didn't know much about bringing up a daughter," supplied Georgianna cheerfully.

"A young lady needs someone other than

28

servants to keep her company, miss. If your poor lady mother could see you now. 'Tis a crying shame that the master never married again. Lord knows I've tried to do my best for you, to do what your mother would have wished."

She got no farther. The girl slid from the table throwing her arms round her generous waist, hugging her impulsively.

"Oh, Batesy, what would we have done without you?"

"Oh, you'd have managed somehow," retorted the woman gruffly, but touched nonetheless. Such a pretty, warm-natured girl was Miss Georgie, not an ounce of unkindness in her, and when you thought of what the poor child had had to endure. Losing her mother so young and then having a father who spent most of his time closeted in his library, ignoring the child, and allowing her to grow up in the care of servants. It was a wonder she had turned out as sweet-natured as she had. The image of her mother, that was what the girl was. Never one for introspection, it occurred to the housekeeper that perhaps it was this very likeness to her long-dead mother that made Sir John shun his only child. Well, whatever the reason, it was nothing short of cruel. In her opinion the sooner this Marquis came and took charge of her and put her in her proper setting the better. Not that she wouldn't miss the girl. She sniffed loudly, hiding her emotion.

"Like I said, Miss Georgie, it was all very well for your papa, a man can manage on his own, but a young girl needs a mother."

Georgianna bit her lip anxiously. "Will my

guardian be very disappointed, Batesy? I have tried my best to learn as much as I can, but I fear I am sadly ignorant of the ways of society."

Instantly Mrs. Bates cursed her runaway tongue. The child was so absurdly sensitive. Of course, it was all her father's fault. If he had taken a bit more interest in her, helped her a little, given her a little love and attention.

Her face softened. "You're a lady right enough, miss, there's no one who could doubt that."

Honesty warred with a desire not to hurt the girl. "'Tis a pity, though, that you have so few ladylike accomplishments. You ought to be playing the pianoforte, and doing embroidery, not dusting and helping me. It's all wrong. I well remember your mama. In the afternoons she would call for the carriage. I mind it well. There she would be, in one of her pretty gowns, carrying her parasol, looking like a picture, going to visit the gentry." Mrs. Bates sighed again.

Georgianna's silvery laugh filled the room. "Dear Batesy." She wrinkled her delightful small nose. "Even if I wanted to play the pianoforte I could not, it needs tuning, and as for sewing, why, you well know I can barely set a stitch." Carefully she avoided mentioning paying or receiving calls from her neighbors.

After the death of his lovely young wife the Squire had become something of a recluse, refusing the sympathetic and well-meant offers of assistance from the wives of his acquaintances in such a manner that they had soon ceased to make them. The years had gone by with Georgianna growing from a solitary childhood to lonely young womanhood with nothing to guide her but her own instinctive breeding, and Mrs. Bates' sketchy recollections of how a young lady ought to behave.

Even as she was laughing, Georgianna was thinking sadly that even if she were brave enough to call on any of the local gentry, in her present shabby state she was more likely to be sent round to the back door for scraps than received in their drawing rooms. She glanced distastefully at her flowered tabby, now tight and shabby from its constant washings, a faint shadow in her eyes. No one but she knew of the loneliness and doubts she hid behind a bright smile, her fear of being rejected, as she had been by her father, and this intense longing she had to be loved and in turn give her own love. Not even to Mrs. Bates could she confide the longing and dread she had for this guardian her father had appointed. Nightly she prayed that he would like her, that he would give her all that her father had withheld, that he would want her as her father never had. She was a sensitive girl, and even while she had resolved not to mind, she could not help but be aware of her father's exclusion of her from his life.

Mrs. Bates shook her head. The Squire had been a good man in his way, none better, but she had never understood how he had been able to neglect his only child so. To be sure, he had seen to it that she could read and write, even supervising her lessons himself occasionally when he realized how quick and intelligent she was, but always in such a cold manner, never hugging her or playing with her as other men did with their children, and yet always ready to frown or scold when she made a mistake.

Georgianna stood with her back to the table, a small, slender girl with a dainty figure, perhaps a little on the thin side; with a charming heart-shaped face, silvery ringlets clustering round her neat head, eyes of a deep, intense blue, now fixed on the housekeeper.

"Poor Papa, if only I had been the son he really wanted, perhaps he wouldn't have fallen into such a green melancholy when Mama died. He loved her so much I don't think he had the heart for anything once she was gone."

It was indicative of her whole character that she was able to say this quite matter-of-factly, without the slightest trace of self-pity, as though it were quite normal for a father to leave the upbringing of his only child to his housekeeper.

They lived very quietly at the Manor. Most of the rooms that had once been filled with music and laughter were now closed up, their furnishings draped in holland covers, gathering dust, and left to grow shabby. Georgianna could not remember the last time they had had a visitor, apart from the Vicar and Papa's man of business. She sighed, her mind once again on her guardian.

"I wonder what the Marquis will look like, Batesy. He will be about my father's age I suppose?" Seeing that Mrs. Bates did not seem disposed to argue, Georgianna brought forth one of her most cherished hopes.

"Perhaps, he might have children," she began hesitantly. "A daughter of my own age, do you think?"

Mrs. Bates saw more than Georgianna would have wished her to.

"Aye, that would be a good thing, miss. That's what you need, company of your own sort, pretty clothes, balls, beaux."

The prospect of such a dazzling future brought a slight flush to Georgianna's alabaster cheeks.

Mrs. Bates smiled kindly. "Why, I remember when your mama was alive. There were dances then, and balls too, the house was always full of people. We had a couple of dozen inside servants alone, not like it is now. People used to come from miles around, and how your mama loved it all. Pretty she was, just like you, and how your papa doted on her."

Georgianna listened, chin resting on her hands. She could barely remember her pretty mother, who had died so young, just a faint recollection of a light, silvery laugh, and a sense of warmth and happiness. Unconsciously she echoed the older woman's sigh. How different things might have been if her mama had not died. Still, it was no use repining. At least she had her guardian. The thought was distinctly comforting. It had not been pleasant to discover that she was completely alone in the world. No matter how much Papa had ignored her, at least he had been there.

"Yes, your mama was a real lady," continued Mrs. Bates fondly. "Everyone loved her. You are the very image of her, miss. At least," she amended, "you would be if you were dressed properly."

Georgiana smiled ruefully, glancing down at her faded, shabby gown. It was three years old. She and Mrs. Bates had made it when Georgianna was fifteen, and she was turned eighteen now, but Papa had never seemed to notice that she was growing up. She had never liked to ask him for money for mere feminine fripperies. There had been some talk of an unfortunate investment. Georgianna did not know the details, but suddenly half the servants had been dismissed and one wing of the house shut up. Papa had become grim and even more withdrawn, a small frown constantly creasing his brow. Almost as though she followed the trend of her thoughts, Mrs. Bates continued.

"Like I was saying, miss, it ain't proper, you eating here in the kitchen like a servant and wearing dresses that a farmer's daughter wouldn't be seen in."

"That's all very well," returned Georgianna matter-of-factly, "but what else can I do? If I eat in the dining room the food is cold by the time it gets there, and besides, I get lonely."

There was an undertone in her voice that touched the older woman's heart. In some ways she was such a child still, despite her eighteen years, and yet in others she had a maturity that was painful to see in one so young, a faint shadowing in her eyes that had no right to be there, a soft vulnerability about her mouth that caught at the heart.

The housekeeper sighed. She wouldn't have credited the Squire with the forethought to provide the girl with a guardian. Why, half the time she had fancied he had forgot her very existence, but still it was just as well he had. She only hoped this Marquis wouldn't prove a disappointment. She knew without being told how much the girl longed for a home and a family. Still, something good was bound to come out of it. This Marquis was bound to move in the very first circles, and Miss Georgianna was such a very pretty girl. Underneath her sensible exterior Mrs. Bates had a very large streak of romanticism, and as she worked she was picturing a most satisfactory future for her young charge, featuring a charming young man and a comfortable, well-provided-for future.

A rather hesitant voice broke in upon these thoughts.

"You do think . . . you do think he will like me a little, don't you, Batesy?" Her face softened.

"Like you! Bless you, miss, of course he will."

"And his wife. She will like me too?"

Mrs. Bates could not in all honesty feel quite as sanguine about this. She only hoped that if this Marquis did have daughters they were either raving beauties themselves, or still confined to the schoolroom. Georgianna was so without conceit herself she would never be able to understand that a mother might feel justly suspicious of her beauty. The child had a lot to learn about life.

Georgiana, with no suspicion of the thoughts running through Mrs. Bates' head, pondered on the possible appearance of the Marquis and his family, but this pleasant reverie was brought to an abrupt end by Mrs. Bates declaring in exasperated tones,

"There now, wouldn't you just know it. Drat that Jem, he promised me faithfully yesterday that he would go to the farm and collect the eggs. And what do I find? Not a single one. The lazy young devil!"

Knowing what was expected of her, Georgianna picked up the basket from the dresser.

"Never mind, I'll go. It won't take long, and besides, it's a lovely day."

"Not without your bonnet, you won't, Miss Georgie," declared the housekeeper firmly.

Dropping the basket, Georgianna took her bonnet from the peg. If anything it was even more faded than her gown, its once pristine freshness now sadly gone, and its brim rather out of shape. She crammed it over her curls, tying the ribbons quickly. At least it kept the sun off her face, and there was no doubt about it, she had an alarming tendency to freckle. According to the *Ladies' Journal* an application of Denmark Lotion cured this affliction, but even had she the money for such a purchase, the nearest town was a good many miles away, and therefore prevention, even in the shape of her old bonnet, was better than a cure.

She stepped out into the sunshine, the clear light revealing the delicate purity of her features, turning the silver-gilt curls to a glowing halo, making her eyes appear almost purple.

It was a couple of miles to the farm, but Georgianna did not mind. She could walk across the fields, it would be quicker that way, and pleasanter too, now that the sun had taken the early-morning dew off the grass. It was a lovely day, the sky a pure, soft blue, small, white clouds playing leapfrog with one another, all the vidid greens of spring vying with one another to catch the eye. Underfoot the grass was soft and springy, so much kinder to her thin sandals than the rutted road. Georgianna smiled gently, "Poor Mrs. Bates." She did her best, but Georgianna was wise enough to realize it was far from enough. From the books in her father's library and the *Ladies' Journals* passed on by the Vicar's wife she had garnered enough information to realize the depth of the rift that separated her from other girls her age.

Her steps slowed a little. How she hoped the Marquis and his family would understand and help her. It was dangerous to want anything too much, she warned herself, but to a girl who had not one single relative in the whole world, and who had never known anything but the cold intolerance of her father and the scolding affection of Mrs. Bates, the prospect of a ready-made family was intoxicating.

All her natural optimism and love of life that had been so sadly crushed by her father's death came surging to life. The fields were a vivid emerald green, birds sang in the hedgerows, stopping now and then to watch her with bright, beady eyes, and the sun shone warmly on her back.

How could she be anything but happy?

Her lively imagination busily at work, she had soon provided her Marquis with an elegant London town house, filled with warmth and laughter; and, of course, a comfortable country estate, where, hopefully, she would soon be safely esconced, and in this delightful manner the farm was soon reached.

Georgianna swung into the lane. The basket with its precious burden of eggs was heavy, but she barely noticed. A bemused smile on her face, she was lost in a happy daydream wherein her guardian, the most delightful gentleman imaginable, was assuring her that he wanted nothing more than to add another girl to his family. Georgianna hoped she had not been an unfeeling daughter, but oh how she wished she might have had a sister, or even a brother, she allowed large-mindedly.

She pushed open the farm gate, humming softly to herself, and stepped out into the road. She started in surprise, her lips parting in a soft "oh." There in the middle of the overgrown and rutted road was the most impressive equippage she had ever seen in her life. What on earth was it doing there? She hurried toward it, noticing the satiny coats of the black horses, champing nervously at their bits, looking very out of place in the quiet country lane. A liveried postillion was peering anxiously down the road in the direction they had come. Whoever it was must be lost. No coaches ever came down this road, it only led to the village for one thing, and for another it was really far too narrow for carriage traffic.

The door of the carriage swung open and Georgianna stood transfixed, unable to move even had she wanted to as she stared at the figure emerging. Her eyes widened. Never in her life had she seen so elegant or handsome a gentleman. Her awed gaze took in the impeccable pearl-gray velvet, the immaculate small clothes, and the quantity of white lace foaming at the vision's wrists. Startled eyes traveled up to his face and stopped, surprising a gleam in the gray depths of his eyes that brought the color surging to her cheeks as she realized that she was staring in a most ill-bred fashion. There was something about the look he bestowed upon her that made her fell distinctly uncomfortable. Why, it is almost as though he doesn't like me. The thought was disquieting. The vision raised his quizzing glass and surveyed her lazily, and Georgianna felt a *frisson* of alarm. It must be her clothes, she decided at length, it was their shabbiness that made him stare so.

At length he lowered the glass and spoke, a vague drawl, yet cool and carrying, "Tell me enchantress, can you direct me to the Manor? I had understood it to be hereabouts somewhere."

He stepped forward, grasping her chin lightly with long, firm fingers. Seen close to, he was even more overpowering. Georgianna was aware that her heart was thudding somewhat uncomfortably. She was not used to being in such close proximity to strange gentlemen; still, she stared trustingly up at him.

He tapped her on the chin. "The Manor, child, where is it?"

A cold secret dread was spreading slowly through her body.

"The Manor?" She was unaware of the slight tremor in her own voice.

The gentleman sighed. "You are perhaps a parrot that you must needs repeat my every word, but there no matter, doubtless you do not know where it is."

As he turned to go, her indignant voice halted him.

"Of course I know where it is, but what do you want with the Manor?"

It seemed to Georgianna that his whole face darkened, and instinctively she stepped back.

"Tell me, child," he inquired softly, "have you never been taught not to question your elders?"

A rich tide of embarrassment suffused the pale cheeks. Georgianna was aware of the titters of the liveried lackeys, and her sensitive soul shrank from the man's cool scorn.

"You mistake, I only asked because . . ."

"Because it is in the very nature of women to be curious," supplied the vision. "Now quickly, child, I do not have much time and even less patience. This Manor, where is it?"

Georgianna quailed a little. His very impatience only served to increase her own embarrassment.

"You have just come past it, about a mile or so down this road."

"Road." One eyebrow rose mockingly. "My

dear child, this cart track bears as much resemblance to a road as I do to the Queen of Sheba. I'm surprised every bone in my body isn't broken after the rattling I have just received. Now tell me again: Where is this place?"

Hesitantly she did so, flushing with fresh mortification as he declared in astonished amusement,

"What, you mean that overgrown place with the rusted gates, that's the Manor?"

Georgianna suppressed a wave of shame that this impeccable stranger should need to speak so disparagingly of her home. The drive was neglected and the gates were rusty, but with only one old gardener and a ten-year-old boy, what else could they do? What time the old man had was spent in the kitchen garden, for Mrs. Bates said, rightly enough, that it was more important to eat than to keep the drive free for carriages that never used it.

As she strived to hide her chagrin, the coldness in the pit of her stomach grew. There could only be one reason for this gentleman inquiring the way to the Manor. She glanced covertly up at him from beneath lowered lashes. He looked cold and uncompromising. She shivered despite the warmth of the sun. In a voice barely above a whisper she asked tentatively,

"Are you the Marquis of Rossington?"

There was a moment's silence. When at last she nerved herself to look up, it was to find herself staring into infathomable gray eyes.

"And if I am?"

Georgianna could not bear to look at him.

"Nothing, 'tis just that you are not what I had expected." Or hoped for, she could have added, but did not.

"I see. And why, pray, should you have expected anything?"

She was too miserable to notice the cold edge of mockery to the words.

"I am your ward," she told him, "Georgianna Lawley."

"My ward!"

Gently he propelled her toward the carriage.

"Are you indeed, and you say I am not what you expected. Well, Miss Lawley, you may tell me of your expectations on the way to the Manor."

With an adeptness she had yet to learn, he allowed her to see nothing of his own surprise.

Once inside the carriage, sitting gingerly on one of its delicate blue-velvet seats, terrified lest she should dirty it with her gown or her basket, Georgianna struggled to master her dismay. This man was so different from anything she had imagined, so cool and distant, surely there must be some mistake?

Something of what she felt must have shown in her face, for he startled her by drawling softly, "I am the Marquis, child."

Was there a hint of softening in his voice? Eagerly she leaned forward with reckless disregard for the eggs, "Forgive me, please, 'twas just that I was so surprised. I had expected you to be much older."

In someone else the remark could have

been flirtatious, but from Georgianna it was merely puzzled.

"And you are disappointed that I'm not?"

In her innocence she missed the cynical undertone, trying to answer as honestly as she could, for her upbringing being what it was, she had no notion of guile, save a reluctance to hurt the Marquis' feelings.

"Well, I own you are not quite what I had hoped for."

There was a small stifled gasp from the man sitting opposite her. He paused in the act of withdrawing his snuff box from one capacious pocket. "Indeed, then may I be permitted to know exactly what you had in mind?"

Seemingly unaware of the veiled sarcasm and the frankly disbelieving look he bestowed upon her, Georgianna hurried on breathlessly, "Well, I had expected you to be more of an age with Papa."

It was a matter that had been puzzling her from the moment she realized who he was, and now she braved his cold stare to inquire gravely,

"Perhaps you were both at the same school, was that it?"

After one swift, incredulous glance into completely guileless blue eyes, the Marquis intoned.

"Hardly."

Georgianna risked another question.

"Perhaps your elder brother then?"

"You are perhaps attempting to jest, Miss Lawley. I am not renowned for my sense of humor or my patience."

Georgianna bit her lip, trying to smile brightly.

"I'm sorry, it is just that it is so hard for me to understand. Why should my father have made you my guardian?"

"You think it is not fitting?"

Puzzled, she tried to understand.

"It all seems so strange."

"Indeed, but the fact remains that you are my ward."

Georgianna saw her dreams rapidly disappearing. She made one last despairing clutch at them, risking a renewal of the cold voice and dark look.

"Do you have any daughters?"

It was plain even to her that the Marquis was taken aback. He searched the small face for a trace of guile and finding none was obliged to reply, "No, did you think I might?"

Georgiana bent her head so that he should not read her disappointment.

"I had hoped you might. You see," her voice was wistful, "I have been vastly lonely."

Another man might have felt a flash of pity, a compulsion to reassure what was obviously a shy and frightened child, but the Marquis merely opened the delicately enameled snuff box and drawled languidly,

"Fascinating, pray continue."

Georgianna flinched as though he had struck her, but continued bravely, "I hoped you and your wife would take me to live with you. I . . ." She broke off in bewilderment as she saw his expression of incredulity. The snuff box snapped shut.

"Have I said something wrong?"

In a very dry voice he told her, "My dear child, I neither have nor do I intend to have a wife, and to the best of my knowledge no daughters of yours or any other age."

"Well, no, I don't suppose you could have," she admitted, "for you would have needed to be married very young, wouldn't you?"

As his eyes rested on her face, Georgianna felt he was probing the very depths of her soul, but for all that, she withstood his glance bravely.

"How old are you, child?"

The question was a surprise.

"Eighteen."

He leaned forward. "I am one and thirty. Methinks I would have needed to be an extremely precocious boy indeed to have produced a daughter your age." He had the satisfaction of seeing a rich tide of color mantle her cheeks, but nevertheless she replied,

"I had thought you to be older somehow."

There was a trace of coquetry in the words. A man less cynical might have found himself stirred to prove how little difference there was between eighteen and one and thirty, but Justin Saint-Vire had known so many women and endured so many carefully baited traps that he had forgotten what true innocence was.

He merely bestowed upon her a look of faintly derisive mockery that Georgianna was at a complete loss to understand.

To own the truth, she was not sorry when the Manor loomed up in front of them. Much as she wanted to like her guardian, there was something about him that made her feel vaguely uncomfortable. It was as though he was waiting for her to do something, but what she could not imagine.

Holding her basket carefully before her, Georgianna gave her hand to the flunkey and stepped out.

"I'll take you to Papa's study; you will have to forgive the bareness, but you see we haven't been using the rooms."

Quickly she ushered him through the hallway, into the old-fashioned paneled room, all at once uncomfortably aware of the shortcomings of her home with its peeling paint and faded walls. The bookshelves gleamed as much as polish and hard work could make them, but many of the books were in a bad condition, their leather covers faded by the summer sun; that same spring sun cruelly revealing the shabbiness of the room, the worn patches on the carpet, the furniture carefully positioned to hide the worst of it, the curtains at the windows that had hung there for twenty years and had suffered badly from the ravages of moths.

"I'm afraid I cannot offer you any wine," Georgianna began formally, but her apologies were waved aside.

"Tell me, do you live here alone?"

She hastened to reassure him. "Oh no, Mrs. Bates, the housekeeper, lives here, and there are three girls who come every day from the village.

"I see. You must live very quietly then?"

She could not see where his questions

were leading, but they made her vaguely uncomfortable.

"Yes."

"No doubt you had hoped your guardian would bestow upon you the benefits normally enjoyed by young ladies of your station in life?"

Georgianna's discomfort increased. It was impossible to miss the sarcasm in his voice.

"I had hoped my guardian might make me welcome as a member of his family."

"To take the place of your father. No doubt the two of you were very close?"

Georgianna had no intention of telling this man of her father's lack of affection for her. Much as she craved it, she could not beg him for what her own father had denied her. Instead she made no reply.

He had his back to her now, staring out across the untidy garden.

"It might interest you to know, child, that you were not the only one to receive a surprise. You see, you too were not quite what I had expected. I believed you to be a boy!"

He swung around so quickly she did not have time to control her features, and so he saw quite plainly the hurt and fear in her eyes.

"And now you see I am not, you do not want me." It was a statement rather than a question. Was it always to be the same? she thought dully. Would no one ever want her? Was he then another such as her father?"

"It is not a matter of 'wanting,'" he corrected her, "simply that it is not fitting for me to take you into my household."

"But you are my guardian."

Their eyes met and held. She would not plead or beg, but he must surely see her need for him.

"And you still want me for your guardian, even though there is no place for you?" he asked softly.

Georgianna kept her head bent so that he should not see her pain.

"You are all I have," she told him simply, as though it explained everything, and for a second she thought she saw a flash of something deep within his eyes. Surprise? Disbelief? She could not tell, but whatever it was, was quickly gone.

He turned from her again, and when he turned back he reminded her of a bird of prey, dark and vengeful, and embittered.

"Very well, if that is what you want."

For a second, gratitude overrode every other emotion. Delight shone from her eyes; with an inarticulate murmur she covered the distance between them, the glowing face lifted trustingly to his.

"You mean I can come with you, you really want me?"

"Oh yes, I really want you."

In her joy, she did not think to question the words or the twisted smile that accompanied them.

"We leave for Paris then in the morning."

"Paris?"

"Paris has been my home now for a number of years." He paused for a second. "Well, child, do you still come with me?"

"But of course. You are my guardian."

Once again that enigmatic glance raked her face, as though searching for something.

"Impulsive child, you do not fear to put yourself in my hands then?"

Georgianna checked, puzzled by something in his voice she could not understand.

"No."

When she looked up the dark eyes were hooded. She was appallingly innocent this ward of his, and would suit his purpose excellently. He glanced downward into the face as beautiful and as fragile as a flower and thought of his mother. His mind was made up. Georgianna perceived his cold smile and wondered at it. If only he was a little warmer, a little easier to aproach. It is because you are not a boy, she consoled herself. At least he will take you, it could be worse. Perhaps in time he would come to care for her, if she tried very hard to please him.

"So it is settled then, we leave in the morning, and now I should like to see Mrs. Bates."

Thus dismissed, Georgianna hurried to the door, pausing for a second, her bottom lip caught between firm white teeth.

The Marquis, correctly interpreting the look raised his eyebrows.

"Yes, child, what now, you have perhaps had second thoughts? You find you cannot bring yourself to overlook my regrettable lapse in not providing myself with a daughter?"

Georgianna gave him a quick, shy look. "No, no such thing, It is just that I am not sure how I ought to address you. I was thinking perhaps . . . I might call you uncle?"

One penetrating glance assured him that she was perfectly serious. Georgianna waited anxiously. Was she perhaps being too familiar?

For once the Marquis was surprised out of his habitual cynicism. Many women had wanted him to be many things in his life, but this was the first time one had ever requested him to be her uncle. His face hardened. If the chit thought to cajole him in that way she was sadly mistaken.

"Don't be ridiculous. You will call me Justin. Most people use my French title, Saint-Vire, as you will doubtless discover, but in view of our, er, close relationship, I think it would be best if you were to be a little less formal."

"Justin!"

Georgianna made no attempt to hide her surprise. She could never bring herself to call this imposing gentleman by his given name. Firmly and forever she closed the door on her dream of her guardian and his hoped-for family. This was the reality, this tall, dark man who looked at her as though he found her faintly annoying.

"You do not care for the name perhaps?" he inquired silkily.

Hastily Georgianna collected her wits sufficiently to assure him that on the contrary, she found it a most excellent one.

"You relieve me, child," she was told laconically. "I doubt if even my reputation could survive the strain if it were to become commonly known that you were wishful of calling me uncle."

Not sure whether he was laughing at her, she looked reproachfully across the intervening space, and instantly saw his face hardening again.

"Well, are you going to stand there all day?"

The change from cool amusement to curt anger bewildered her.

"I . . ."

"Tell this Mrs. Bates I wish to see her if you please, and prepare yourself for the journey. You will need a warm cloak."

He did not proceed, but from the way he glanced disparagingly over her gown, Georgianna guessed the direction of his thoughts.

With a haughtiness that would have surprised those who knew her, she returned his look with one of her own.

"But of course, I shall wear my winter one."

As she prepared to stalk from the room, hard fingers closed over her own. "Let us understand one thing before we start, my child, and then perhaps we shall deal very well together."

As he paused she glanced warily up at him. His fingers were bruising her own with angry pressure, and she had the added disadvantage of having to tip back her head to meet his eyes.

"I am not prepared to countenance childish tantrums and defiance. If you wish to indulge in them, you will not do so in my presence."

No threat of punishment accompanied the words, but her eyes fell, and when she walked

from the room it was with a defeated step.
Halfway down the passage, optimism reasserted
itself. Paris! All the precepts of ladylike behavior forgotten she ran pell-mell up the stairs,
humming happily, determinedly ignoring the
faint antipathy that seemed to emanate from
her guardian.

Chapter
3

The journey to Paris, undertaken with such high hopes, ended on something of a sour note for Georgianna.

Her first intimation that all was not well came when she awoke from the light doze she had fallen into shortly after they had left the pacquet. The Channel crossing had been particularly rough; unpleasantly boisterous waves had sent the boat rocking like a barrel in a millrace, and the combination of a night without sleep and the cool, fresh breeze coming off the water had had its natural effect.

She had been leaning against the Marquis' shoulder, her eyes firmly closed, her breathing light and easy, oblivious to the use she was making of this most convenient prop. Cold, thin sunlight danced across her face, highlighting the delicate bone structure. The man at her side glanced down into the sleeping face, and perhaps it was as well that Georgianna was unaware of his scrutiny and unable to read his thoughts. Idly he wondered how many people, knowing him for what he was, would believe she was merely his ward, and how long after that before the whispering behind fluttering fans became a roar. His mouth tightened slightly. It was no part of his plan to have the girl's reputation torn to shreds by the vixens of Versailles; quite the reverse.

The carriage jolted and the fair head slipped farther into the warmth of his shoulder; Georgianna came to with a slight start, awareness returning like a flood tide. She glanced at her companion. The averted profile was not encouraging, neither were the compressed lips, but even the first faint stirrings of alarm could not totally obliterate her happiness. She struggled to sit up, straightening her gown and bestowing a glowing, half-shy smile upon her guardian.

"I hope I did not discommode you?" A faint blush accompanied the words. The appeal was ignored. There was no response from the man at her side, save a cool glance.

"If you had done, be sure I would have woken you."

Dismissed, she turned to the window, but it appeared he had not finished. "Still, now that you are awake, there is something I wish to discuss with you."

Thick lashes veiled her eyes. Georgianna had an uncomfortable suspicion that for her at least the discussion was not going to be a happy one. She folded her hands neatly in her lap and waited.

"You realize, of course, that it would be quite improper for you to live with me without a chaperone?"

Georgianna, who had not given the matter much thought, shook her head. Perhaps already he was wishing he had left her in England. The thought was enough to bring fresh shadows to her eyes.

"You do not care for the idea of a chaperone?" The words were edged with faint *hauteur*, but Georgianna still retained enough spirit to reply, albeit a little pleadingly.

"But you are my guardian!"

"My dear child, you surely cannot expect me to rearrange my whole life to suit you?"

He heard the smothered gasp, but merely continued smoothly. "You can scarcely have thought we were going to live an idyllic life *à deux?"*—

An inarticulate murmur and tightly clenched hands were his only response, and for a second Georgiana had the quite unaccountable impression that he had deliberately set out to wound her.

"I do not want a chaperone," she told him quietly, trying not to betray the depth of her hurt, for while it was true that she had not given much thought to her life with the Marquis—after all, there had scarce been time—she was not foolish enough to suppose he would always be able to be with her. There must be many demands upon his time, but when he had spoken she had gained the impression that he did not want her company—which surely must be ridiculous for if that was the case, he would not have brought her with him?

"No? But then you see, my dear, it is not your wishes that count."

She stared at him in dismay. Why was he behaving so coldly toward her? Had she angered him in some way?

"You do still want me, don't you?"

"But of course. Are you not the daughter of my father's best friend?"

Georgianna tried to feel reassured, wishing she might understand him better and that he would unbend toward her just a little more.

Suddenly reaction set in. Every bone in her body ached with fatigue. Her eyes felt gritty and her hair untidy while the Marquis lounged easily in his seat, moving comfortably with the motion of the carriage. He looked as impeccably groomed as when they had set out, indeed almost as though he had stepped straight from the hands of his valet. The thought, so ridiculous, brought a small smile to her mouth.

"Something amuses you?" asked the Marquis.

"Er, no."

"Well, to continue with this matter of your chaperone. I have the very person in mind, the Comtesse du Farnand. She is a relative of mine, a widow."

"Will she not mind?" Georgianna asked doubtfully. "I mean, having to leave her own home?"

The Marquis was not accustomed to people querying his decisions.

"Mind? Why on earth should she?"

His drawl became more pronounced. "On the contrary, I fancy you will find her an extremely willing accomplice, especially when it comes to spending my money on new finery."

"Finery?" Her brow creased. "Oh, you mean clothes!"

Under his mocking glance her color deepened.

"Oh you cannot mean for me! You could not buy my clothes, it wouldn't be proper."

This fresh evidence of naïveté seemed to amuse the Marquis, and for the first time Georgianna saw him smiling, albeit rather faintly.

"My dear child, I hate to contradict you, but I most assuredly can and will. You are my ward and you will be dressed accordingly."

Georgianna fell back against the cushions, her eyes wondering.

"I can scarcely expect Claudine to present you at Versailles dressed as you are now, even if she were prepared to, which I doubt. Ridiculous child, if I don't provide you with clothes, who will?"

Color surged into the pale face.

"I'm sorry you find my clothes so, so wanting," she announced stiffly. "Doubtless my present appearance is a great source of embarrassment to you." Far from seeming annoyed by her words, he merely laughed.

"Embarrassed! You will soon learn that that is impossible. I care not the slightest what the world thinks about me."

Happiness welled up inside her, like a fountain suddenly fed with water, so that her eyes sparkled and her lips parted in a happy smile.

"Is it then because you care what the world thinks about me?"

She was swiftly disillusioned. "Well, shall we say that it is far more important for you to retain your reputation than it is for me to try to regain mine."

"It is?"

"But of course. Otherwise how will you make a good match?"

"A good match?"

The fountain of joy gave way to a cold, insidious fear, a helpless, nervous feeling, as though she were standing at the top of an icy slope.

"You mean you want me to get married?"

"But of course," came the silky response. "Isn't it the ambition of every young lady, a rich, titled husband? Not of course that we can hope to provide you with both. After all, with very little portion of your own, I think the best you can hope for is the title. Not that I would send you to your husband dowerless, and with so many of these old titled families needing to marry money, I shouldn't wonder if . . ."

"Don't, don't, please!"

The hateful words washed over her on a wave of disbelief. She could barely credit that she was hearing aright.

The dark face portrayed well-bred surprise.

"You cannot mean you would pay someone to marry me?"

The Marquis permitted himself to indulge in a little gloating. "How could you achieve a good match otherwise?"

Matches, doweries, of course she wanted to marry someday, but not in this cold-blooded fashion, like inferior goods carefully disguised to hide their flaws, she thought on a spurt of indignation.

"Ah, I see what it is, you had perhaps some girlish daydream of marrying for love. Is that it?"

She could not bring herself to respond to the indulgent teasing. Suddenly it was all too much. This glittering figure who was her guardian, the high-handed manner in which he disposed of her future, his apparent unawareness of the many small wounds he had already inflicted upon her. There was a large painful lump in her throat, and only by the greatest effort and blinking hard several times was she able to prevent her tears from falling.

He only wishes to do what is best for me, Georgianna reassured herself.

Naturally he expects that I should want to achieve a good marriage. After all, these things are conducted differently in Society, and as for her chaperone, well, of course she would need one. With the self-control and common sense that had stood her in such good stead during her lonely childhood, she concentrated on telling herself how fortunate she was.

Even before they reached Paris, Georgianna could see its outline sprawling across the horizon, the blue sky tinged faintly gray as though a cloud hung over it. A hundred questions hovered on her tongue, but as the Marquis appeared to be sleeping, his dark head turned from her, she had to content herself with staring through the window and trying to supply her own answers. She looked toward him. His tricorn was pulled low over his eyes, his hands in the deep pockets of his coat. What did he really think of her, she wondered? He had told her he had thought she was a boy, and yet he had evinced little surprise at discovering she was a girl. Even in sleep there was an air of hard purpose about him, taut and unrelaxed.

Now the coach was rattling over the cobbled streets, through narrow alleys where the upper stories of the houses nearly touched one another. Then they came out into the wider *faubourgs* where the nobility had built their grand new houses back from the road, the magnificent façades catching at the imagination, standing in a bog of mud and filth that shocked the country-bred Georgianna into uttering a small cry of consternation.

Hastily she closed the window, opened to enable her to get a better look. Her gasp, small though it was, was sufficient to wake her companion.

"Unpleasant, isn't it? But you will grow accustomed to it. They say that the Parisiens are a religious race, their eyes are always fixed on the future and Heaven, and thus they are able to ignore today and the hell that lies beneath their feet."

The gurgle of laughter that greeted this sally was not quite what he had expected. The keen gaze sharpened a little. Could it be that Miss Lawley was not the boring little country mouse he had thought?

Georgianna, her spirits somewhat restored by this evidence of good humor, ventured to ask a few questions.

"Don't they ever clean the streets then?"

"Never," came the calm reply. "You are lucky you are seeing it for the first time on a dry day. When it rains the streets become a sea of mud. I have seen coaches bogged down to the axles in it, and duchesses lifting their skirts above their knees to avoid ruining their finery. As you will soon discover, none but the very poor walk in Paris."

"And yet you choose to live here."

"Choose?" It seemed his good humor had deserted him.

"Well, you do have a home in London."

She wondered at his harsh laughter, drowning out the rattling of the carriage over the cobbles as they swept on through the gray dusk of the late afternoon, the coach never checking as it traversed the narrow streets at a pace little short of reckless. The Marquis, she was later to learn, was not a gentleman who appreciated wasted time.

At last they stopped, and to ears now accustomed to the rattle of wheels over cobbles and the sound of horses' hooves, the silence seemed strange.

"We are here. Let us hope you do not find your new home as disappointing as your new guardian."

Georgianna opened her mouth to deny the accusation, and then closed it sharply. She was beginning to feel somewhat out of charity with her guardian. She still hadn't forgiven him for his comments concerning her possible marriage. She darted him a sideways glance and decided upon the instant that any gentleman who proposed to marry her must be willing to do so without the benefit of a dowry.

As the massive door was thrown open, the

blue-and-gold livery she was coming to recognize was very much in evidence. A footman of impressive magnificence bowed low, and with the unobtrusive efficiency produced only by immense wealth, the travelers were ushered inside.

Her clothes might be shabby, and she might not be used to the ways of Society, but Georgianna was determined not to let her fear show. With her head held as proudly as any satin-clad duchess she swept forward, graciously allowing a lackey to remove her ancient cloak, and stiffling a small giggle at the expressive twitch of his long nose as he bore it away. She looked toward the Marquis, wanting him to share her amusement, but if anything he looked even more aloof than the footman.

"Jacques, my ward, Miss Georgianna, will want a room. See to it. Oh and have a room prepared for my aunt, Madame la Comtesse."

The major-domo might have been with his master for a dozen or so years, he might have fancied himself inured to his strange ways, explaining them away to the rest of the household with a Gallic shrug and a fatalistic *"Anglaise!"* But, despite all this, he was unable to prevent his jaw dropping and a slightly glazed expression affixing itself to his face.

However, he knew better than to pass comment especially when he saw the gleam in his master's eyes.

"Er, yes, the Peacock Room?"

For a moment the Marquis seemed to hesitate, but when he spoke his voice was quite firm.

"No, the room my mother used to occupy!"

This time, Georgianna's delighted cry covered the other's surprise. "You are giving me your mother's room. Oh how kind you are!"

The major-domo hastily recollected himself and bestowed an extremely frosty glance upon other members of the household, who were all staring with varying degrees of astonishment at their master.

The Marquis, quite aware of the breathless interest of his household, contented himself with a cool smile.

"Jacques will show you to the salon. If you will excuse me I shall just pen a note to Claudine."

The journey over, Georgianna's natural spirits began to reassert themselves. To be sure it was a great pity that her guardian was not disposed to be a little more approachable, and in fact she had to admit there had been occasions when he had appeared distinctly distant. But then no doubt it was as strange for him as it was for her, and she was being allowed his mother's room, which proved that he must have understood a little of how she felt. She resolved to dwell no further on the matter, but to wait upon the development of events.

The Hotel Saint-Vire was as different from Rossington House as it was possible to be. Successive generations of Saint-Vires had carefully added lovingly chosen treasures to the rooms so that lacquered Chinese cabinets rubbed shoulders with inlaid marquetry tables. Sevrès ornaments perched next to carved jade figures. The salon was decorated in shades of pink and cream. Georgianna, blinking in delighted wonder, thought she had never seen such beauty. She glanced up at the ceiling, dazzled by its intricate plaster-work, and then down at the floor, where lavish cream roses enhanced the dusty pink softness of the magnificent Aubusson. Panels of pink silk bordered with gilt adorned the cream walls; gilt-legged chairs covered in rose and cream damask waiting invitingly.

Georgianna had the fancy that in a room such as this it would be impossible for strife to exist; the room seemed to reach out and enfold her. From the wall a laughing girl looked down at her, her white shoulders exposed in a swath of pink satin, and two cream roses nestling in her hair.

"My mother." He had entered so quietly that she had not heard him.

"She was very lovely. You must miss her very much."

"Yes, I do."

Georgianna could almost have sworn the broad shoulders had a quietly despairing air, and averted her eyes with exquisite tact, yet still she could not help catching a glimpse of the shadowed face in the enormous gilded mirror. With a womanlike urge to comfort, she offered, "At least you had her until you were nearly grown. I can barely remember my mama, although Mrs. Bates says we are very much alike."

As though something in her words disturbed him, the Marquis moved away, shrugging aside her sympathy.

"I imagine it might be some hours before

Claudine arrives. It would be as well if you were to rest for a while. One of the maids will show you to your room."

Georgianna, who until that moment had been feeling rather tired, took immediate exception to the curt command.

"No, I am not tired."

Blue eyes challenged gray, and then fell.

"Oh, but I think you are."

She opened her mouth to protest vehemently and realized the futility of it.

"Well, perhaps I will have a rest.

"Most wise," agreed the Marquis. "I am delighted to see that we understand one another. I should be reluctant, but not, you understand, averse, to using force, should it become necessary."

Outraged, Georgianna stared at him.

"You mean you would make me go to bed? But you can't, I'm not a child."

"No? Then do not behave like one; so far I have seen little evidence that you are anything else."

The gibe brought angry color to her cheeks. Her guardian was most definitely not improving upon acquaintance. One moment he wanted to marry her off to the first man to offer for her, and now he was ordering her about like a schoolroom miss.

The straight line of her back was eloquent with disdain, but nevertheless she obeyed his command.

Despite her very natural annoyance Georgianna could not repress a small start of delight as the maid showed her into her room. The woman smiled broadly when she saw the girl's expression.

"You like it?"

"It's lovely," breathed Georgianna. Gently she touched the pale blue satin cover on the bed. Her guardian's mother had slept here. That dark head of the portrait, so reminiscent of her son's, had lain against those very pillows. A little of her anger flowed away.

The maid was talking again. "Mademoiselle must be tired. I shall instruct a girl to bring up some hot water so that you may refresh yourself." She was gone in an important bustle of silk skirts, leaving Georgianna alone in her new domain.

Holding a branching candelabra in one hand, she toured the room. It was quite exquisite. Silk panels, painted in the Chinese fashion, hung on the walls. Soft, glowing, jewel colors against a pale blue background, depicting flaunting birds of paradise. The same silk-covered chairs so delicate she fancied she would be frightened to sit on them. Idly she traced the outline of a pagoda with one finger. She had thought the salon a lovely room, but this defied description!

She was still moving slowly through the room, touching here and there with reverent fingers, when a couple of maids returned with the hot water. A delicately lacquered screen was discovered to be concealing a hip bath, and before too long Georgianna was soaking in the luxury of warm, scented water.

The two young maids, new recruits to the

Saint-Vire household, managed with creditable aplomb to assist their new mistress into a gown far inferior to their own. Georgianna was about to ask a few pertinent questions, mostly about the Comtesse du Farnand, when a discreeet knock interrupted.

Without needing instruction, one of the girls opened the door a faint crack, and then returned with a message.

"Madame la Comtesse has arrived and awaits you in the salon!"

Descending the stairs in the wake of the flunkey, Georgianna tried to quell the nervous flutters invading her stomach. The man indicated to the half-open door and left.

Uncertainly, Georgianna moved forward. From outside the room she could hear voices. The lady's was faintly reproving.

"*Tiens,* Justin. What is all this? You drag me away from Versailles, just in the middle of the best on-dit I have heard in years, with some mysterious note about wards and chaperones. The role of guardian will not sit easily on your shoulders, I vow."

And then the Marquis's voice, laconic and bored.

"If you would just allow me to explain, Claudine."

Unwilling to eavesdrop any further, Georgianna gathered up her courage and entered.

"Lud, Justin, is this your ward? You wretch, you give me all manner of stupid detail and then you never tell me the most important thing of all. She is quite beautiful. Come here, child."

Georgianna needed no second bidding.

Madame la Comtesse was not as she had imagined at all. Even with her hair dressed high and powdered, her arms and bosom sparkling with diamonds, and gowned in a creation that quite took her breath away, she still retained the warmth that had made her popular all her life. Claudine du Farnand had never been a beauty, neither had she many accomplishments, but yet her salons were always well attended. She had never lacked an escort, and when she had married one of the most eligible prizes in Versailles, no one had been really surprised. Ambitious mamas with plain daughters comforted themselves with recalling how much she had achieved with little more than their own offspring. But Claudine had a gift more important than mere beauty and far more lasting. She had a genuine love and interest for her fellow men and women, a kind yet brisk attitude that could make nonsense of the most desperate of tragedies, and a warmth that drew people to her to bask in its healing comfort.

She opened her arms and without the need for words, Georgianna ran into them. With the saving grace of laughter she turned to her nephew.

"Justin, you rogue, you knew I should not be able to resist her. You know how I have always longed for a daughter."

Only an awareness of her guardian's silence, and, she was sure, mocking scrutiny prevented Georgianna from indulging in a hearty burst of tears.

Madame hugged her fondly and then put her from her.

"Poor Justin, he does not understand how it is with us. These men."

Gray eyes, more than a little reminiscent of her nephew's but a good deal warmer, smiled down at her.

"Poor child, you look exhausted, we have much to discuss, but it can wait until tomorrow. Come give me a kiss."

Shyly, Georgianna did as she was bid. Already her heart was lifting. The Marquis may have fallen far short of her imaginery guardian, but the Comtesse! She was all and more than she had ever dreamt of.

If Georgianna had been privileged to witness the scene taking place between aunt and nephew once she had quitted the room she would have been extremely surprised.

The Comtesse did not waste time. Eyes just as penetrating and quite as merciless as the Marquis' own were turned in his direction.

"Well, Justin?"

The Marquis, who throughout the interview with Georgianna had been lounging against the wall in an attitude of careless elegance, replied mockingly,

"Well what, Claudine?"

"Not what?" she corrected mildly, "but why? I understand how the child comes to be your ward, but what I fail to understand is why you have brought her here."

The elegant shoulders shrugged. "Because it was my duty."

Aunt and nephew exchanged a long and unsparing look.

"Duty, you, *non*. I only wish I could believe it, but I know you too well." The Comtesse paused for a moment, searching carefully for the right approach. "'I should not want to see *la petite* hurt, Justin."

"Hurt, what makes you think she will be? Believe me, Claudine, I have only her welfare at heart. You may indulge your extravagant impulses to the hilt. See that she is properly gowned and presented, and find her a suitable husband."

Madame's eyes sharpened a little. "No, Justin. You have some other deep purpose. I can see it in your eyes. I do not pretend to understand your reasons for bringing the child to Paris. I shall just pray that *le bon Dieu* will forgive you for any harm you try to do her."

"But you will act as her chaperone?"

"And if I refuse?"

The broad shoulders shrugged agaiin.

"She is still my ward, and her place is with me."

The Comtesse gasped in dismay. "Lud, Justin, you cannot mean it. Her reputation would be in shreds within the week."

"As long as that," drawled the Marquis, unrepentant.

"Very well, Justin, I shall do as you ask, although I do not believe my task will be an arduous one. The child will certainly not lack admirers." She paused delicately for a moment. "She is, I can take it, provided for?" Again the careless shrug.

"Her father died practically penniless, but that need not deter you. She will have a good dowry, that I promise you. In fact"—his face seemed to close in, shutting him away with some private dark thoughts—"I shall insist upon it."

There was only one matter left to be broached, and the Comtesse, knowing her nephew as she did, guessed in this instance delicacy would avail her nothing. "Forgive me, Justin, but I must ask you. There will be no danger, I trust, of the child forming a romantic attachment for you."

"You need not fear, Claudine, I have not descended to the seduction of innocents."

"It was the girl herself I was thinking of, not you."

One eyebrow arched in mockery. "Believe me, Claudine, you mistake the matter. I have it on good authority that, in my ward's eyes at least, I figure as nothing more romantic than an uncle, albeit a youthful one, added to which I have the additional handicap of being unmarried and without offspring."

Claudine's mouth fell open. "À *vrai dire*, Justin, you jest!"

"Most assuredly, I do not."

"Tell me more," she invited.

Contrary to what he had given Georgianna to suppose, the Marquis was not totally without a sense of humor, and when he had finished, the Comtesse joined in his laughter.

"Oh poor child, she must have been dreadfully unhappy."

Her nephew, it seemed, was not disposed to agree. "Why should you think so? She seemed quite content with her life. Doubtless her father doted on her."

The comtesse, who was well aware of the ever-open wound her nephew bore, smiled a little sadly and said nothing. On all other matters but those touching upon his own father, Justin was open to reason. His father's treatment of both his mother and himself had warped something in his nature. She knew better than to protest that no caring father would allow his only child to be clothed in an outgrown and faded gown, nor would love and security have necessitated those faint shadows she had observed in the girl's eyes. It would be worse than useless to protest. Justin would not see the truth because for some reason of his own, he did not want to.

Briskly she pulled on her gloves. "So, Justin, it is settled. I have an engagement for this evening but you may instruct the servants to collect my trunks, and tomorrow we shall start on *la petite*'s education."

"I wish you joy of her," came the curt response.

"You have no need, I shall enjoy it vastly," Claudine assured him calmly.

As he followed her to the door, she watched him, puzzled. "You are surely not going out tonight?"

"No, why should I not do?"

"But, Justin, that poor child, all alone."

"Alone? In a house full of servants? You repine too much, Claudine."

Sadly, she shook her head. It would be bad enough if he were merely guilty of not understanding but a more astute male than her nephew she had yet to meet.

Chapter
4

The Comtesse was not one to waste time. No sooner was breakfast over than she instructed Georgianna to fetch her cloak.

It was quite plain to the Comtesse, a woman of considerable experience, that in many ways Georgianna was very young for her age. When she does love, she mused to herself, it will be the *grande passion*. She will give everything she has and not count the cost. Before that time came she hoped the child might be suitable and comfortably married. A discreet affair, conducted behind the protective cloak of marriage, was perfectly convenable, even accepted, but for a young, unmarried girl to indulge in an *affair de coeur* meant ruin and disgrace.

The Comtesse sighed a little. Versailles was like a succession house; Georgianna's beauty and maturity would rapidly come to flower under its exotic roof. It would be her duty to guide and protect her. But first, the child must be gowned! The Comtesse firmly believed in dealing with one problem at a time, and for now she intended to concentrate on a Georgianna who would bedazzle the French court.

Georgianna, dismissed to collect her cloak, returned to the room at the same time as the Marquis arriving from his morning ride. Dressed casually, with his coat held carelessly in one hand, he looked years younger. Georgianna softened toward him, but instantly regretted it when he returned her warm smile with a hint of something she could not quite understand and only knew made her aware of embarrassed confusion.

The Comtesse, who had intercepted the look and was quite aware of its import, frowned reprovingly at the Marquis—she had seen him bestow such a look on coquettish young ladies far too often to mistake it.

"Come, Georgianna, we have much to do."

Indeed they had.

The carriage took them through a maze of narrow, winding streets and alleys, into what the Comtesse patiently explained to Georgianna was the older part of Paris.

Everywhere there were beggars, noisy and frightening in their demands, some running right up to the carriage so that Georgianna was relieved when the Comtesse cautioned her to let up the window.

Georgianna glanced around with interest when they had to stop to allow a groaning water cart to pass, while the Comtesse grumbled a little at the state of the roads. They were heavily congested—even with the carriage window closed, Georgianna could hear quite clearly the cries of *"fouette, cocher"* mingling with oaths and curses.

A couple of running footmen flashed past the carriage, muscles bunching under their livery, and a washerwoman emerged from a house staggering under a weight of laundry. At last they were moving again, drawing nearer to the Palais Royal and its shop-filled arcades, some of which were already causing muted— and, in some cases, not so muted—laughter among those of the courtiers who sought their pleasures in Paris.

Seeing her charge's eyes already wandering in the direction of a window containing discreetly worded advertisements offering wares no young lady should have any occasion to concern herself with, she hastily took her arm. "Those shops are for gentlemen. We shall go this way."

Georgianna, on the point of questioning her, fell silent, her attention mercifully caught by a frivolous display of bonnets in a milliner's window. An hour later, when she fancied they must have entered every single shop in Paris, and her feet were beginning to ache dreadfully, Georgianna was too tired to do anything but agree with whatever the Comtesse saw fit to suggest.

Ruthlessly she was dragged into yet another *modiste*'s. However, this time it seemed that the Comtesse was prepared to be satisfied. Georgianna, her mind already dulled by an endless parade of materials and colors, stared around while the *vendeuse* was summoned.

She arrived in a swirl of satin, looking impossibly grand, dismissing the hovering attendant with the merest lift of an eyebrow.

"Ah Madame la Comtesse," she gushed. "Such a pleasure, and if one might be permitted to say so, a privilege to assist. What is it to be? A new gown? A riding dress?"

The Comtesse drew Georgianna forward. "*La petite* will be making her curtsy at Versailles. She will need to be suitably gowned."

The *vendeuse* sighed in ecstasy.

"*La grande toilette,* but of course. Marie, Josephine, the Chinese silks if you please, *vite!*"

"Would the ladies care to be seated?"

Graciously the Comtesse allowed that they would. Georgianna sank back into her chair with relief, only to start up again when the girls came back with the materials. Not even in the fashion plates in the *Ladies' Journal* had she imagined such fabrics. She caught her breath. Surely no one would ever dare to wear a gown made from such exquisite stuffs. But apparently they did, for the Comtesse laughed away her half-murmured protests.

A bolt of blue satin shimmered across the table, delicately embroidered in silver-and-blue peacocks, with flaunting tails, the eyes shimmering strangely. Georgianna bent to touch one. "It's real," she declared wonderingly.

"Silly child, what did you think it would be—paste?"

Over her head, the Comtesse and the *vendeuse* exchanged amused looks. "Miss Lawley has only recently arrived from England," supplied the Comtesse graciously.

"Ah, *Anglaise*. Might it be permitted to ask if miss is a relative?"

"Mademoiselle is the ward of my nephew, the Comte de Saint-Vire."

The black eyes of the *vendeuse* snapped. Monsieur le Comte. One had heard of him, of course—a most formidable gentleman. She rolled her eyes, and gave Georgianna a shrewd look. The Comtesse knew quite well that before the day was out all of Versailles would know of Georgianna's arrival.

The formalities thus disposed of, the ladies turned their attention to the important matter of clothes.

"You like the blue then, child?" the Comtesse asked.

Georgianna nodded her head breathlessly. There were not words to describe how much.

"Tis well enough, but not for your presentation gown, of course," murmured the Comtesse disparagingly.

Flowered tabbies, silver tissue, figured velvets all passed before Georgianna's bemused eyes. Surely she would never be able to wear all of these garments?

Sensing her charge's thoughts, the Comtesse said gently, "You will need them all, child, and more. At Versailles it is sometimes necessary to change one's gown a dozen times a day." She was aware, however, of her charge's reluctance to indulge in the type of spending orgy normally so dear to the female heart, and palliated. "Of course, it is not purely for your benefit, there is Justin to think of. It would go ill for him if people were to say his ward was not well turned out."

Georgianna was not quite as green as the Comtesse had imagined, and an old-fashioned look from clear blue eyes told her as much.

To a person who had sometimes wondered where the next meal was to come from, such reckless spending on clothes was difficult to adjust to. Still, she had to own it would be pleasant to see that faint disparaging glance disappear from her guardian, and even more pleasant to see it turned to startled admiration. Before she even had time to banish the thought as uncharitable, two velvet riding dresses and an armful of muslin morning gowns were added to the steadily growing pile.

It seemed to Georgianna that every one was more dazzling than the last, delicate hand-painted Chinese silk, heavily embroidered satins, gowns trimmed with row after row of expensive lace, all with matching underskirts and delicate, fragile slippers.

Apparently satisfied, the Comtesse turned to the waiting *vendeuse*. "Now for *la grande toilette*."

"Certainly. Perhaps something very simple for the young lady. I think I have just the thing. Something that will draw the eye and yet retain her air of fresh charm."

Feeling extremely embarrassed, Georgianna wished they would not discuss her as though she were an inanimate object, but her embarrassment was forgotten as the woman returned with the material. It was silk, but so fine and so delicate it seemed like gossamer, and it was plain white.

She lifted it toward the light, and both the Comtesse and Georgianna caught their breath. It was embroidered with a strange thread that was at once colorless and yet under the lights flashed with a thousand myriad colors.

"It was brought to me," the *vendeuse* explained, "by a merchant with whom I have dealings. It comes from China, and he smuggled it on board his ship. He told me that it is a material that is worn only by their princesses— and he certainly charged me dearly for it!" she grumbled.

"It is beautiful," announced the Comtesse firmly, resolutely ignoring the exorbitant sum of money the woman whispered to her.

Saint-Vire could afford it, and the Comtesse intended Georgianna to benefit from the full measure of his purse, to compensate in some small measure for the indifference she sensed within him for his ward.

However, she communicated none of this to Georgianna, and that young lady, rendered speechless by all the munificent bounty that had come her way, raised shining eyes to tell her: "I cannot wait to thank my guardian." The Comtesse, smiling a little grimly, hurried Georgianna out toward the carriage. "You like Saint-Vire then, child?" She had waited until they were settled against the comfortable velvet before asking the question.

Georgianna tried to answer as honestly as possible. Did she like him? she wondered. Truth to tell, she did not know. She wanted to, she wanted to pour out to him all the affection that had been damned up for so long, and yet she sensed he would reject it if she did. "He has been very good to me," she offered cautiously at length.

"You are a sweet child, Georgianna. Perhaps later I shall tell you a little of his story. Life has not always been kind to him, and if you find him a little hard, or a little difficult to understand, you will perhaps make allowances?"

"I shall try to," came the honest reply. "But sometimes it is very difficult." Madame laughed heartily and agreed that this was so. "Still," she continued in a brisker tone, "perhaps it will not be long before he is no longer your guardian?"

"You mean if he sends me back to England?"

"*Non, non.*" Madame saw her fear and hastened to reassure her. "I mean when you marry. With your looks, I vow St.-Vire will find himself beseiged with suitors for your hand. The French are not like your cold Englishmen, you know."

"But they will not take me unless he gives me a dowry."

Once again shrewd gray eyes rested on the dainty profile, and Georgianna had the uncomfortable suspicion that the Comtesse was reading her thoughts with unpleasant accuracy.

"And that bothers you? Silly child, it is the custom."

Thus Madame disposed of the fears that

had kept her awake half the night. It was not as she had imagined at all. Far from wishing to humiliate her, her guardian merely wished to provide for her future. A little of the rebellion that had been growing steadily ever since they had left the pacquet faded.

One day followed fast upon the heels of another, with Georgianna mercifully seeing little of her guardian. Yet on those occasions when she did she could not help but be aware of a strange tension in the air. Whenever his eyes chanced to rest upon her he seemed to be challenging her pride.

He came into the Rose Salon that the Comtesse had claimed as their own, just as Georgianna was showing off some of her new finery. He flung himself into a chair and observed their looks of surprise.

"This is still, I believe, my home?" The Comtesse shrugged. She disliked the gleam in his eyes.

"Well, well, my charming ward. Come here!"

Georgianna glanced doubtfully at the Comtesse. Georgianna had come downstairs, well pleased with the effect of rose silk, cunningly draped to reveal a heavily embroidered cream underskirt. Her curls tumbled loosely around her shoulders, shimmering with gray powder.

"Go to him, child," the Comtesse ordered kindly.

Obediently she did as she was told, trembling a little as hooded eyes raked her face.

A few paces away, the Comtesse watched

anxiously. Georgianna had seen Justin in this mood too often before to trust him to behave as he ought. One wrong word, one feminine attempt to cocquette, and she would probably find herself dismissed as crudely and curtly as any woman of the streets.

"So . . ." His lip curled slightly. "Can this really be the same girl I found standing in a cart track not three weeks back?" His eyes lifted to his aunt. "You are to be congratulated, Claudine."

Under his hands Georgianna trembled a little, as much at the tone of his words as at the touch of his fingers on her skin. She sensed he was under some great strain, and unknowingly provided the final straw.

"My gown is very pretty. It is a little like the one your mama is wearing in her portrait."

Three pairs of eyes rested on the portrait. Georgianna then turned to look at her guardian and almost fell back in alarm at the look of fury and rage upon his face. Only the pressure of his hands upon her shoulders prevented her.

"I'm glad you fancy there is some similarity, for it won't be long before you find yourself sharing the same fate."

"Justin!" The Comtesse's warning came too late. While Georgianna stared at him in surprise, cruel fingers dragged her across the room until she was standing under the portrait.

"She wasn't laughing the last time I saw her, neither was she looking so pretty. That portrait was painted when she was seventeen, just before her marriage to my father. Only a year younger than you. She died before she was thirty." Impossible not to be affected by the words, Georgianna shivered. With an abruptness that sent her reeling, she was released. Without another word the Marquis was gone, only the echo of the slammed door left to remind them that he had ever been present.

Georgianna took a deep breath. "Why? I do not understand." Claudine du Farnard sighed. This was a moment she had hoped to avoid a little longer.

She patted a small stool at her feet, and when Georgianna had settled herself, carefully spreading her skirts to avoid crushing them, she took both her hands in her own. "It is not a long story, Georgianna, but a rather sad one, although not really uncommon. Justine was devoted to his mother and blamed his father for her death."

"How did she die?" she asked curiously.

"Of neglect or a broken heart, it is impossible to say."

She told the story simply and quickly, and when she was finished, the young girl's eyes were soft with tears.

The Comtesse touched her face. "Do not waste your pity on Justin, child, he does not need it."

She saw no need to burden the girl further by telling her of the debauched career her nephew had embarked upon after his quarrel with his father, or explaining to her the manner of man he had become.

She didn't need to. Georgianna was gifted with imagination. She could fill in the intervening years for herself, and cried fresh tears for all that might have been had he not become so embittered.

"So you see, you must try to be patient with him, child."

Neither of them mentioned the strangeness of his wishing to keep Georgianna with him, nor his ever-increasing tendency toward sarcastic and hurtful comments.

Chapter
5

Summoned downstairs to give a display of the curtsy she had been practicing so assiduously, Georgianna paused decorously outside the salon door. She gathered up her skirts and received in the process a rather appreciative smile from a bronzed running footman adorning the hallway. Jacques, while joining the rest of the household in adoring its latest occupant, was not prepared to permit such familiarity, and the footman was dispatched to the kitchens.

Clutching her gown nervously, Georgianna waited for the lackeys to throw open the doors. She then started in dismay. Oh no, not her guardian. It was too late now to back out. He had seen her and was wearing that cynical look that she hated so.

From the shadows the Comtesse's warm voice was encouraging. "Come in, child. Justin, you can be Louis."

Georgianna quelled a small nervous giggle. She would rather curtsy to a dozen Kings than to her guardian. She saw by the look in his eyes that he was expecting her to flounder, to miss her step, and the look challenged her.

She was wearing the blue silk, its shimmering beauty no lovelier than the eyes it matched, the peacock's eyes catching the light as she swayed gracefully toward the waiting man.

The Comtesse, while giving the appearance of being totally engrossed in her stitchery, looked on, willing her charge to have confidence.

It must have worked. She stood quite still in front of him, and then gathering her skirts sank to the floor in a pool of blue silk, the fair head bent over the outstretched hand in deep obeisance.

The Comtesse ceased to ply her needle; even the faint ticking of the clock seemed to fade. They made a startling picture—the girl's pose revealing her soft, vulnerable neck, the man's eyes unguarded and brooding. For a second the Comtesse almost fancied he was about to stretch out his other hand and touch the girl's neck, but he checked and announced coldly,

"Passable; now for the hard part. Let us see if you can rise." Indignantly, Georgianna rose with perfect grace and timing. Passable, was that all he could say? Hot words trembled on her lips, quenched as she caught the Comtesse's warning finger.

He was impossible. It was useless to try to please him. However, the culprit seemed blightingly unaware of chagrin.

"She will do, Claudine."

Georgianna looked anxiously from one face to the other.

"You will arrange for her presentation then?" the Comtesse asked.

"I have already done so," came the laconic response. "It is for tomorrow."

"But you hadn't even seen my curtsy," said Georgianna.

"You have been practicing it these ten days past. It would be strange indeed if you had not perfected it by now."

Thus he robbed her achievement of all its pleasure. Unable to find the words to express her anger, Georgianna took refuge in a feminine ploy as old as time itself, only this time accompanied by an offended fluttering of the fan that she clutched in her left hand.

As the door closed behind her, the Comtesse gave way to her laughter.

"Poor Justin, but you cannot blame her. That was most unkind. She has been practicing that curtsy so carefully, and I own she does it very creditably. You might at least have complimented her upon it, or is that not part of your 'duties'?" she inquired with heavy sweetness.

"It is certainly no part of them to pay the child compliments. If that is what she looks for, she must look elsewhere."

"Compliments!" Claudine's expression was droll. "You talk as though you are expected to deliver a positive barrage of them, when all that was needed was one, and a well-deserved one at that. I quite agree that there's no necessity for swelling the child's head, that will doubtless be achieved without your assistance, but to speak to her so."

She saw by his slight frown that she had had her revenge.

"She will take then?"

"My dear, can you doubt it? One only has to look at her. All Paris will be at her feet, she will be inundated with suitors."

"Even when it is learned that she has no portion?"

"Ah yes, that was not well done of you, Justin."

"What?"

She did not allow herself to be provoked; years of dealing with her nephew had taught her the folly of it.

"You know what. Telling the child you would have to 'buy' her a husband."

"She complained to you, did she?"

The Comtesse's heart missed a beat as she saw the savage satisfaction in his smile.

Inwardly she cried out against his expression, but outwardly, with her normal calm composure, she shook her head. "Of course she did not complain. Why should she? She thinks it is merely another instance of your 'kindness.'"

Saint-Vire crossed the floor and stood beneath the portrait of his mother, staring broodingly up into the laughing face.

"And you, Claudine, you do not think I am 'kind' to my ward, despite the depradations I have allowed you to make upon my fortune?"

She refused to be baited. "You already know my views, Justin. I have always considered you to be a very astute person. You do yourself less than justice if you persist in this folly, and I warn you, in the end it will only be yourself who suffers."

"You don't think then that I might possibly cause my charming ward some suffering along the way?"

With a calmness she was far from feeling, the Comtesse busied herself with her sewing. "*La petite* has her own protection, Justin, as I think you will one day discover. The pity of it is that by that time it will probably be too late, and now if you will excuse me."

She packed away her silks without haste, her own eyes just as ironical as those of her companion. Just what fate her nephew had in mind for Georgianna she did not know and would not ask, but she had learned enough about the girl and her life, to know that her brave spirit would rise above anything that could be used to hurt her. Anything but love, a small voice warned; she had no protection against that. She reflected, with a trace of her nephew's cynicism, that the guardian angel of innocence must indeed be working hard on the child's behalf. So far she had remained strangely unaware of Saint-Vire's magnetism. The Comtesse offered up the pious hope that she would continue to do so.

"Marie, is my train straight?"

Georgianna craned her neck around anxiously in a vain attempt to see behind her.

"Mademoiselle is *ravissement*," came the reassuring reply. "*Très belle*. And now, if you will allow me, this ringlet I think—so!" Tongue protruding a little, Marie stood back the better to judge the effect of her work, her expression admiring, as well it might be.

Georgianna was indeed *très belle*. The magnificent Chinese silk had been made up into a gown of surpassing beauty, yet combined with artful simplicity that emphasized her fresh youthfulness. The gown was completely free of lace or knots or ribbon, simply opening over a silver-tissue underskirt, the delicate white material looped up here and there to reveal the tissue, the loops caught up in a shimmer of diamonds. The bodice was cut square and to Georgianna's eyes a little on the low side, embellished with a row of bows marching down to the narrow pointed waist. However, it wasn't until she moved that Georgianna saw the full beauty of the gown. The silk, as delicate and light as a spider's web, billowed with every movement of her body, shimmering and swaying, as though the fabric possessed a life of its own, glittering with a thousand different and changing colors, like sunlight trapped in a diamond.

Marie stepped forward and gave the ringlet nestling against one white shoulder a judicious twitch before pronouncing herself satisfied. There, she was quite ready. Now her fan, where was it? Ah yes, and her perfume? Patiently she waited while Marie sprayed her.

Initially, when the Comtesse had told her of the custom at Versailles for all the ladies of the court to wear the same perfume, she had been surprised. In order to appraise her of the sense of the rule, the Marquis had said: "If they did not, the place would stink like a whorehouse."

It was plainly obvious that the Comtesse was none too pleased by her nephew's frank assertion, nor by his following remark: "I'm sure by now Georgianna must realize such places exist." He had directed a cynical look in her direction. "I trust my frankness does not offend your maidenly ears?"

"On the contrary," she had been able to retort calmly, but she was grateful to him nonetheless, for she had not been aware that such places were the subject of polite conversation.

Even now recalling his faint start of surprise brought a smile to Georgianna's lips, that even the icily curt remonstrance that had followed her outburst had been unable to completely squash.

Today the perfume was to be bergomot, its slightly sweet overtones making Georgianna wrinkle her nose.

"That's enough, Marie, it's far too heavy."

A final glance in the mirror, an anxious twitch of her skirts, and Georgianna was ready. Marie bustled forward and nodded to the footman. The door was opened, and with fluidity that comes only from natural grace, Georgianna was through it. She paused for a second, one hand on the bannister, and peered down into the hall, feeling self-conscious all of a sudden. Resolutely, she placed one small foot on the stair, held her head high, and then with an upsurge of confidence swept forward.

The door of the Rose Salon was open. At

first she thought it was empty and then she caught a flicker of movement. Her guardian! She glided in noiselessly and thus had ample opportunity to observe the full glory of his raiment.

He was wearing a balldress in cloth of gold, the fabric taut across his back, flaring out into the stiffened skirts. At his side rested an ornate dress sword, glinting wickedly as the light touched upon it. He was staring silently through the window, although what he could hope to see she could not imagine, for it was quite dark outside. It was obvious he was unaware of her presence. His long white fingers rested lightly on the polished surface of a small chest, emeralds winking on their elegant slenderness like fathomless pools of deep green water.

As always when she entered the room, Georgianna glanced at his mother's portrait, sympathy suddenly outweighing her animosity. Impulsively she walked toward him, not stopping until she had reached him.

"I haven't thanked you yet for my gown."

She was near enough to catch the rattle of his swift indrawn breath and the faint widening of his eyes as he swung around and saw her. For a moment neither of them spoke; Georgianna had the strangest impression that from her portrait his mother smiled beneficently down upon them. There was a look in her guardian's eyes that was neither mocking nor indifferent, and then it was gone.

"You don't like it?" Her question was anxious.

"Like it?" Smooth as silk he told her, "My dear, there isn't a man alive who would not like it, or its contents."

Rosy color flooded Georgianna's cheeks. The Comtesse had just entered the room and overheard the remark. She shot him an incredulous look. A compliment was one thing, but a comment that bordered on the flirtatious was quite another. However, it soon became apparent that this was a day for surprises. The Marquis, it seemed, was prepared to lay aside his normal guard. From his coat he produced a long oblong box, flicked open the catch, and removed its contents.

Georgianna caught her breath at the river of fire and light that cascaded through his fingers, and knew without even looking at her that the Comtesse echoed her sigh.

"Come, turn around."

For a moment she could only stare. Then, apparently tired of waiting, the Marquis walked toward her.

His warm breath fanning the back of her neck gave her a strange shivery feeling as the cold metal slid against her skin.

"No, don't touch it," he warned. "Wait until I have fastened it, and then you can look."

There was a muttered oath, and for a second Georgianna fancied the fingers brushing her skin had trembled a little.

"There, it's done!"

Georgianna shivered as she stared at her reflection. The necklace was like no other she had ever seen. Strands of gold so fine as to be almost flexible were woven into the shape of delicate flowers, diamonds forming the petals; the whole was fashioned in such a manner that even the lightest breath set the diamonds trembling, throwing out prisms of light. Never in her life had she imagined owning anything so lovely. For a second tears misted her vision, and then they were gone. Gratitude welled up inside her, and careless of Madame's warnings and her own instincts, she hurried toward her guardian. Quite what she intended to do when she reached him she did not know. However, he stepped back, his whole aspect forbidding and warning her to go no farther.

"Dear me, such enthusiasm, and all for a few baubles. Your husband will have cause to be pleased with you, especially if he is the donor."

The words were uncalled for, and his aunt's expression told him so as she strove to soften the blow.

"Justin knows you are grateful, child. But he is right; you cannot embrace every gentleman who gives you a gift."

It was no good. She had been humiliated, and all three of them knew it. From that moment Georgianna resolved to give the Marquis no furter opportunities to criticize her gratitude. From now on she would be more circumspect. But still the damage was done, and the memory of her action and his rejection of it kept a hectic flush of color in her cheeks long after Paris had been left behind them.

The journey to Versailles was not a particularly pleasant one; with several hundred carriages jamming the roads it could not be otherwise, but at length they were there. A hovering lackey removed their cloaks and then they were joining the vast, milling crowd. Despite the problems occasioned by her own lack of inches, by keeping her eyes fixed firmly on the Marquis's broad back, Georgianna managed to plunge after him, marveling at the manner in which the crowd parted to let him through.

They traversed a series of cold and lofty antechambers, arriving by she knew not what route in the Marble Court. From there they proceeded up an ornate marble and gilt staircase, so crammed with bodies that she held her breath, fearful lest her gown be crushed. By the time they were halfway up she had completely lost sight of the Comtesse, and it was all Georgianna could do to keep her foothold on the stairs. Georgianna stared around, dazzled by the amount of gilt and ormolu; the vastness of the court, and the glitter from the thousands of tapers, were faithfully reflected in the vast sea of jewels. Her awe had apparently not gone unnoticed, and it only took a sardonic glance and a recollection of the earlier scene to bring the color storming back into her cheeks.

"Come!"

To her amazement her guardian drew her forward, one hand comfortingly under her elbow as they crossed the hall and hurried through another series of chambers. Halfway through one, heavily encrusted with a deal of gold paint and crimson velvet, and to Georgianna's mind nowhere near as attractive as the Rose Salon, someone stopped them.

"Saint-Vire, I didn't know you were back in Paris." The newcomer stepped back to stare in surprise at Georgianna.

"You have missed me then, Conde? How very flattering."

The man was about the same age as her guardian, his hair well powdered and his blue velvet decorated with an impressive array of stars and orders. He laughed a little at the lazy drawl, quite as though he were used to it, Georgianna reflected.

"Faith, Saint-Vire! One thing I certainly have not missed and that's losing to you, but Paris is a dull place without your enlivening presence." He switched his gaze back to Georgianna, staring at her in a manner that brought a renewal of the drawl.

"Well, Conde, since you are here, allow me to make my ward, Miss Georgianna Lawley, known to you."

"Your what!" The quizzing glass, which only moments before had been held in the languid fingers, dropped unregarded to swing ignored from its velvet ribbon. "*Dieu*, Justin! You jest!" exclaimed the young man piously, his expression changing as he caught the soft gleam in cool gray eyes.

"Ah, forgive me, you do not jest! Miss Lawley."

He made her a magnificent leg while the Marquis drawled, "Child, the Prince de Conde."

Georgianna, engrossed in her curtsy, did not see the look that passed from black eyes to gray, and that was faultlessly returned.

"So, you are presenting *la petite* to our good Louis?"

"Indeed. The Cabinet du Conseil, I believe."

"Yes, the court is gathered there." Conde pulled a wry face.

"If you want something more entertaining, the gaming tables have been set up in the old Oeil de Boeuf, but for myself I shall be going to Paris once I have done my duty here." He paused for a moment.

"Oh by the way, Phillipe du Plessis is here somewhere!"

"I thought Louis had banished him?"

Conde shrugged. "He had, a matter of du Francine's daughter, but that has all blown over now. You know, Philippe, he has charmed La Pompadour into pleading for his return."

The Marquis's lip curled faintly. "He must indeed have been desperate if he needs to go to such lengths."

Conde laughed. "You know Philippe."

"Oh indeed, something of a connoisseur where the fairer sex is concerned."

Georgianna looked from one man to the other. Who was this Philippe that he should merit such a dark look from her guardian?

Conde laughed again, looking down into her puzzled face.

"He is no more a conneisseur than yourself, Saint-Vire. Still, if you are wise you will guard this particular treasure from his ardent gaze. Or perhaps that is what is in your mind, eh my friend. You fear lest he should steal her from you?"

"Hardly," came the brief reply. "I doubt my ward has the ability to attract du Plessis' eye, or that having attracted it she could hold it!"

Georgianna seethed with anger; Conde was less restrained.

"You think so. I fancy you are too sanguine, *mon ami.*" He shrugged aside the words.

"Miss Lawley, perhaps you will be kind enough to save me a dance. And now, Miss Lawley, Saint-Vire, I have the honor to take my leave of you."

With a flourish he was gone, soon to disappear in the mingled rainbow of silks and satins, leaving Georgianna alone with her guardian and her temper. If he was aware of her feelings, he ignored them.

"It seems you have made a hit with the First Prince of the Blood, child, but do not, I beg, place too much importance on a few idle compliments."

"Oh, you mean he will not really wish to dance with me?"

It was not what he meant at all, and his measured glance told her so.

Fortunately, for Georgianna at least, the Comtesse, having fought her way through the crush, had sighted them at last. "Ah Justin, there you are. Well, *petite?* I saw Conde talking to you. Did he ask you to dance? If he should deign to notice you . . . He is quite charming, don't you think?"

Georgianna tilted her nose in the air, in no way disposed to do what was obviously expected of her and admire the young man. "Certainly, he seemed very pleasant," she agreed. "But quite ordinary."

"Lud, child, a Prince of the Blood, and you call him ordinary. Justin," appealed Madame.

There was a definite glint in the cool gray eyes now. "You will refrain from calling the Bourbon heir an ordinary young man, if you please. It is not becoming in you."

Despairingly Georgianna wondered what was, and the Comtesse, fearing an open outbreak of hostilities, hastened her forward.

"Justin, we must go to the King, it is time."

It seemed to Georgianna that the vast, cold chambers would never end. One was set out with card tables and chairs and she took this to be the Oeil de Boeuf mentioned by the Prince. A couple of others were set out with large tables, groaning under the weight of food on them, and so packed with people that it was impossible to see how anyone could eat. At last they reached the far chamber; the Swiss Guards standing by the door stood back to allow them entry, and firmly the Comtesse piloted Georgianna forward. At the far end of the room, by the fireplace, was a cluster of people.

Nervously Georgianna stared around. Which one was the King? As though sensing her dilemma a firm hand touched her on the shoulder. Thinking it to be the Comtesse, she glanced up and found to her astonishment that it was her guardian. Of course, his concern was not for her, she told herself wryly; she had learned that much by now. It was probably lest she disgrace him by making her curtsy to the wrong person.

Happily no such disaster overtook her. She sank down into her curtsy, her gown billowing out around her like a swan's feathers.

His Majesty was disposed to be very gracious. He bent over Georgianna's hand, one curl of the perriwig unnervingly close, the small, shrewd eyes assessing her as he welcomed her to the court.

She kicked aside her train with fluid grace, and made her turn, justly proud of the manner in which she managed to accomplish the difficult maneuver, and then at last it was over. The Comtesse was at her side, smiling and full of praise. With her was Saint-Vire, dark and silent.

"Excellent, *petite*, all eyes were upon you, weren't they, Justin? There can be no doubt, you will be a success!"

She then hurried Georgianna forward, not giving her a chance to reply or to wonder if momentarily she had seen a glint of warmth in her guardian's eyes.

"Now, the ballroom. Justin, you will partner her for the first dance?"

Georgianna opened her mouth to protest that she did not want to dance with him, and then closed it in a hurry.

"I believe my ward considers me too decrepit to risk even the cotillion, Claudine. Is that not so?"

All at once Georgianna recalled Madame's assertions that her nephew was something of a rake, and suddenly for the first time she could give the thought credence. She knew instinctively that to perform any dance with the Marquis would be a heady experience, but still one that she did not want. Her experiences with him to date had not led her to believe that he would look kindly upon missed steps and awkward feet.

Realizing that he was waiting for an answer, she replied with quite tolerable composure, "You tease me, I think. I expect there are any number of ladies who would be delighted to dance with you."

"But you yourself do not number among them, is that it?"

The silky tones warned her that she was on dangerous ground.

"But it isn't the same thing, is it? I am only your ward, it is a matter of duty rather than pleasure."

He gave her an extremely percipient stare -and then drawled, "You would have it otherwise?"

This had the effect of totally oversetting her hard-won poise. A soft blush, followed by delicious confusion, told him quite plainly that the arrow had found its mark.

The Comtesse judged it time to take a hand.

"Ah, but it will not always be so, Cherie? I predict before this night's out, he will find he cannot get a dance with you."

Suddenly the ballroom was before them, and there was no time for anything but a startled gasp as the crowd carried them forward. Along the whole of one wall were immense mirrors that reflected every angle of the vast ballroom, so it seemed as though there was an infinite sea of swaying, brilliant color. On the other side of the room arched a succession of windows flanked with intricately carved and gilded pillars, soaring up to the vast painted ceiling upon which Le Brun had depicted the Grecian gods at play. There was hardly any furniture at all in the room, merely a collection of small tables and a few chairs. But in view of the crush of people, Georgianna fancied it was probably as well.

Overhead hung enormous chandeliers, each one containing over a hundred candles, their light trapped and thrown back by the mirrors, until the whole room was awash with color and light. The mere volume of human voices was nearly sufficient to drown out the musicians; here and there she caught the odd snatch of conversation, drawled, well-bred, arrogant, while the cream of French Society paraded before her, like a peacock unfurling its tail.

They were barely in the room when a familiar figure joined them. It was the Prince de Conde.

He gave a neat bow and then led Georgianna onto the floor. It was hard to believe that this charming man with the mischievous smile was really of royal blood. The reality was soon brought home to her, however, as the people moved to make way for them.

"Why have they stopped dancing?" she murmured softly, puzzled at the gust of laughter that rocked her companion.

"They wait for us to begin."

"Us?" Her hand flew to her mouth. Oh how could she have been so foolish? She had been told that no one may dance until a member of the royal family gave the signal to do so. Her cheeks were scarlet with mortification, but it appeared that Conde, far from being offended, was merely amused. She tried to picture her guardian's reaction to the same situation and was relieved it was Conde she was with and not him.

The Marquis was dancing too, and Georgianna thought he looked exceedingly fine. It was obvious that she was not alone in thinking that, for his companion, a pert redhead of somewhat ample charms, was using every excuse the dance presented to allow her person to touch his, and when denied that opportunity fell back on the lure of pouting lips and soft glances.

Until Conde coughed politely in her ear, Georgianna was not aware how often her eyes had returned to the other couple.

"I expect like everyone else you have conceived a *grande passion* for Saint-Vire?"

The words were light enough but Georgianna, uneasily aware of the dangerous drift of her own thoughts, renounced the idea quite thoroughly. "He is my guardian and nothing more. He doesn't even really like me."

"No?" Conde shot her a considering look. "'Tis certainly a strange situation in which he finds himself—Saint-Vire of all people to be the guardian of innocence."

He saw he had gone too far and with great delicacy turned to a less explosive topic of conversation. However they were words that were to be repeated in one form or another all evening.

Left on her own with a glass of rather indifferent wine, Georgianna could not help noticing that her guardian was dancing with the redhead yet again. Not that she herself had been lacking in partners, far from it, but all were carefully scrutinized by either the Comtesse or Saint-Vire himself so that they were as tepid as her watered-down wine.

Through the crowd she caught a glimpse of shoulders quite as broad as the Marquis' own, only these were topped with a head as silvery as her own rather than the more familiar black hair. Encased in rose brocade, the shoulders forced a path through the crowd. Eyes of a vivid and intense blue swept the room. At her side someone bumped into her, and her glass fell from nerveless fingers. When she looked up the man was standing at her side, his eyes startled and appreciative. Something about their admiring warmth lifted Georgianna's failing spirits. "You are all right?" His voice was husky and concerned.

She thanked her rescuer, bestowing upon him a faintly roguish smile.

"The wine wasn't very nice anyway, so I'm not sorry to have lost it."

"No? And there was I hoping I might be permitted to bring you a fresh glass."

In the face of such naturalness it was quite easy to take the proferred arm. The gentleman was all charm, and Georgianna remembering an earlier conversation ventured to put a question to him:

"Do you happen to know Philippe du Plessis?"

The fair head inclined slightly toward her, the blue eyes looking into her own. "You have some special reason for asking?" enquired her cavalier carelessly.

"Oh no, I just wondered if you could point him out to me. My guardian says he is a connoisseur of women."

"Really, and you perhaps wish to have his seal of approval?"

He saw by her expression that she did not fully understand.

"No matter," he told her easily. "You wish him to admire you, is that it? To have this distinction of capturing his heart?"

"Oh no!" Georgianna hastened to assure him, adding honestly, "Besides, I doubt I could, for my guardian says that even if I did catch his interest, I could not hold it."

Perceiving that he was regarding her with extraordinary gentleness, Georgianna flushed afresh. "Oh dear, I ought not to have said that, ought I."

"It is our secret," he assured her gravely. "Now, as for this matter of Philippe du Plessis, a sad rake by all accounts, I'm surprised your guardian allows you to know his name. Shall I effect an introduction for you?"

"Oh!" She colored again. "I did not . . ." A shy upward glance assured her that she was perfectly understood.

"I tease you, *petite*. I'm afraid I have a confession to make: I am Philippe du Plessis!"

For a second she was struck dumb. "Oh dear!" Helplessly she struggled between blushes and apologies until her companion laughingly took hold of her hands.

"The blame is all on my side."

He leaned forward, a rather wicked smile playing around his mouth. "Permit me to tell you that your guardian is quite wrong. In fact, you are in the gravest danger of having me drop to my feet before the whole of Versailles and offer you my heart."

A small trill of laughter escaped rosy lips, and hearing it, Philippe du Plessis smiled briefly.

The Comte du Plessis had not attained his age of eight and twenty without sampling a good many of this life's pleasures; indeed, his ready indulgence in them was a source of constant despair to his regimented family. He would not for one moment have argued with those who called him a rake, and indeed would probably have cheerfully agreed. Certainly in the past he had been no great respecter of innocence, but there were some things that even he would not stoop to, and looking down into the face raised to his in trusting amusement, he was reminded of them. A strange guardian the child had. Whoever it was ought to be protecting her from him, not practically encouraging her to seek him out. His eyes caressed the small face. Life had been dull of late. With infinite grace he raised Georgianna's hand to his lips, and before she could resist bestowed a lingering kiss on the soft white skin.

"Shall we teach this guardian of yours a lesson, *petite?*" he asked her softly.

Georgianna felt a tiny spurt of amusement. All around them people were staring. She had a delicious sensation of doing something faintly shocking, and yet at the same time infinitely exciting.

Philippe du Plessis, an experienced hunter, saw the look and smiled.

"This guardian, who is he?"

"The Comte de Saint-Vire."

"What! Saint-Vire! Lud, child!"

Why was it people kept referring to her as a child? Georgianna wondered crossly.

"Do you want to get me run through?"

Georgianna shrugged carelessly.

"Oh, Monsieur, my guardian cares nothing for me. Besides," she added sadly, "he would never really believe you would wish to flirt with me, and of course I know there is no question of marriage, for he has already told me that I shall be lucky to make a merely respectable match."

"Has he indeed?"

A quick glance at the drooping mouth and he was cursing the Marquis. What was Saint-Vire about? The girl was entrancing, and he had a good mind to tell her so. He grinned all of a sudden, looking very boyish. "So, it is agreed then. We shall teach Saint-Vire a lesson he will not forget quickly."

Georgianna could not remember agreeing to any such thing, but the idea certainly had appeal. "Do you know my guardian?"

"Of course. All Versailles knows Saint-Vire."

No need to tell the girl that together with a few other young gentlemen of birth and money, he and Saint-Vire formed the nucleus of what the more respectable portion of Versailles were wont to describe as a parcel of libertines. He and Saint-Vire had enjoyed many an unorthodox "adventure" together. He glanced down again at the girl at his side. She was astonishingly lovely, and the mischievous streak that had already led him into a good many unpleasant situations prompted him now. The girl would come to no harm in his hands. Doubtless Saint-Vire had some respectable alliance arranged for her; it was well known that rakes always made the strictest fathers.

Fathers! He glanced at Georgianna again and was convulsed with laughter. There couldn't be more than a dozen years between them. It would be amusing to ruin all Saint-Vire's carefully laid plans; indeed, a course the Marquis himself would probably have embarked upon in different circumstances. He was still grinning hugely as he hurried Georgianna through the crush of people. He stopped once to eye her sternly. "Now, nothing of our conversation to your guardian. You and I have never met, understand?"

Georgianna nodded. Whatever her guardian said, she liked Philippe. He was fun, and what is more, he was all that her starved heart cried out for.

"There you are!" A voice broke in upon her thoughts. It was the Marquis.

She started guiltily, but Philippe was gone.

"We had begun to think we had lost you, child. How did you manage to get over here?"

"Oh I was just watching the dancers, I suppose I must have moved a little."

"Half the length of the ballroom. More than a little, I should say, wouldn't you, Claudine?"

Georgianna was saved from the necessity of replying.

"Saint-Vire!" No one hearing the greeting could have doubted its sincerity, and yet the Marquis' eyes narrowed fractionally.

"Du Plessis."

Georgianna stiffened, not daring to lift her head.

"And your companions? Madame la Comtesse I already know, of course, but . . ." He hovered delicately over the words, glancing at Georgianna.

The Marquis received the words with a cool smile. "This, my dear Philippe, is my ward."

"Your ward? You are indeed fortunate, Saint-Vire!" marveled the other, at the same time making a leg that put even Conde's in the shade. The Comtesse glanced uneasily at Georgianna to see how she was responding to this vision of manly perfection.

Georgianna was trying hard to stifle a giggle as innocent blue eyes were turned in her direction.

"Is it to much to hope I might be permitted to know your ward's name, Saint-Vire?"

"Not too much, merely unnecessary, I should have thought, Philippe."

"You mean you will not permit the introduction?"

A fair eyebrow rose in incredulity equally as disdainful as the Marquis' own.

The Comtesse judged it time to intervene. They were receiving some rather amused stares.

"Georgianna, allow me to present you to Monsieur le Comte du Plessis."

"Philippe," whispered the irrepressible offender.

Georgianna's lips quivered in suppressed amusement.

Very prettily Philippe begged the privilege of a dance, and graciously the Comtesse acquiesced. Saint-Vire maintaned a cold silence, and yet despite the silence, antagonism flared between the two men; Philippe's hold of Georgianna's arm tightened proprietorily; he took a slight step toward her guardian, a hint of tension stretched the air, but then before he could say a word another voice broke the stillness.

"Saint-Vire! And your ward, I do believe. Won't you introduce me?"

The slight tension Georgianna had sensed before was nothing to the explosiveness of the atmosphere that surrounded them now. The very stillness was somehow far more telling than a thousand words.

Her guardian, Madame, and even Philippe seemed frozen in a strange tableau. Georgianna, completely at a loss to understand what was happening, stared at the newcomer. She was one of the most beautiful women she had ever seen. Enormous violet eyes returned her stare. The silence persisted. What was the matter? Who was the lady? A friend of her guardian's or perhaps something closer? She was on the point of sinking into her curtsy when hard fingers gripped her, forcing her to remain upright. The lady's hand was on her guardian's arm, pale and fragile against the cloth of gold. Her silky dark hair was swept back to reveal exquisitely dainty ears, studded with diamonds. There was something in the air Georgianna could not quite understand. The large eyes were fixed challengingly on her guardian's face, and there were faint patches of color in the Comtesse's cheeks, but otherwise she seemed perfectly composed. Philippe was staring into the distance, his eyes cool and wary. The Marquis gave the lady the most distant of bows, his drawl faintly pronounced.

"I regret, Madame, that I am unable to introduce you. You will, I am sure, understand."

His words were plainly audible, and for a moment there was a complete and unnerving silence. The lady then turned on her heel, her delicate skin flushed where before it had been pale, her fingers leaving his arm as though it had been red hot. In her eyes something sparkled. Was it anger? Tears? Georgianna did not know.

Her first instinct was to turn and demand that he introduce her at once, but something in the stance of the others prevented her. Someone, a thin, sallow gentleman, had taken the lady's arm, turning her around and walking determinedly toward the Marquis.

"You have insulted my sister, Saint-Vire, and I demand satisfaction." There was a stunned pause, and then all around them excited chatter filled the air. Only the Marquis remained silent. At length he opened his snuff box, slowly taking a pinch, before closing it decisively, and then he spoke.

"I fear you cannot have it!"

The thin man drew nearer.

"Well, Saint-Vire, it seems that while you are content to insult ladies, you are unwilling to face gentlemen!"

Audible gasps escaped those near enough to hear. The other dancers turned to watch. Georgianna waited, her mouth dry. She understood what was happening; the gentleman had challenged her guardian because he had insulted the lady. But what would the Marquis do? Surely he could not ignore the challenge.

It seemed he could.

His eyes narrowed faintly.

"Monsieur Clary, you are being extremely foolish. To the best of my knowledge no lady has been insulted, and I believe I have never shown myself unwilling to meet any gentleman."

The slight emphasis on the last word drove the color from the man's face. Furiously he turned on his heel, his fingers gripped around his sister's arm. A wave of excited chatter broke out, and Georgianna, knowing full well that her guardian was looking at her, turned to Philippe, her eyes sparkling dangerously.

"I believe, Monsieur le Comte, we were about to dance."

Pointedly, she ignored her guardian. How could he have insulted those people so? She shivered. Wasn't it just like him, though? She recalled the number of times he had hurt her, some of them quite deliberate. That poor woman. How pale she had been.

Philippe, summing up the situation at a glance, bowed gallantly and offered her his arm. Once they were out of earshot, she tugged impatiently at his satin, her eyes dark and stormy. "Philippe, why did he do that? It was unkind."

Philippe du Plessis looked down at the floor and then up into the small angry face. "I think Saint-Vire did not think it proper to make the lady known to you," he began carefully.

Georgianna brushed this feeble excuse aside. "But why?"

She could still not believe it had actually happened. Vividly she recalled the man's hatred and the stricken face of the woman. Surely nothing could excuse such behavior. The incident had quite ruined Georgianna's pleasure in the evening.

"I'm sure you would never have behaved so!"

"No? You think then that I am less of a gentleman than your guardian?"

"Less?"

He patted her arm. Saint-Vire must be quite out of his senses to let this innocent loose on her own.

"It occurs to me that you do not perfectly understand. Saint-Vire and the lady were at one time very good friends."

Comprehension dawned on Georgianna and faint color flooded her cheeks.

"You mean she is his mistress?" she accused.

"Was," amended Philippe. "You surely did not expect him to live like a monk; believe me, it is quite accepted."

"And is it also accepted that he should subject her to such humiliation in front of the entire court?" came the cutting response.

"That was for your benefit, *petite*," she was told gently, while Philippe's amused and sympathetic eyes rested on the flushed countenance.

"Mine!"

"The lady should not have tried to force an introduction to you; it is not done."

"But the Queen acknowledges Madame de Pompadour."

"That," declared Philippe firmly, "is quite different."

It seemed useless to try to explain to this child that to have introduced her to his mistress would have placed her firmly and forever in the same category, despite the installation of the Comtesse du Farnard, and as for the Queen! His shoulders shook a little at the thought of anyone even wanting to seduce Louis' plain and dumpy *hausfrau* from the paths of virtue.

Georgianna was not to be palliated. "But to insult her so brutally," she persisted.

She made an entrancing picture, although she was not aware of it. Her small head was thrown back, her eyes were dark with temper as she subconsciously pleaded with Philippe to agree with her. And Philippe, never a man to resist temptation for very long, had a reckless urge to suggest a promenade in the gardens. Scarcely had the thought formed than, chancing to look toward the doors, he perceived Saint-Vire. A soundless laugh shook him. Saint-Vire was going to have his work cut out with this charming minx, *Dieu,* if he wasn't already halfway to falling in love with her himself.

Georgianna, unaware of the less than decorous turn her companion's thoughts had taken, tried again. "It was brutal . . . and . . . unnecessary."

Philippe sighed. "Try to understand, *chérie.* Had Saint-Vire allowed her to meet you, it would have been an insult to you. He simply could not permit it, not with all Versailles looking on. It was foolish of the lady to try —she knows the rules."

"But what about her brother?" she asked uncertainly. "He challenged my guardian, and yet he refused to meet him."

"Not refused," corrected Philippe. "He is not able to duel with Clary. You see, Georgianna, Versailles abounds with rules made by the King, and the court must abide by them or risk dismissal. Clary knew well enough when he challenged Saint-Vire that it was impossible, or else he would never have done so," he added cynically. "Saint-Vire is a notable swordsman."

"You mean dueling is forbidden?"

Philippe sighed again. "No, duelling is not forbidden, but it is forbidden to duel with persons of inferior rank."

Georgianna absorbed this information in silence and then asked, "And Monsieur Clary is of inferior rank?"

"To Saint-Vire, yes," replied Philippe frankly. "Very minor nobility on his mother's side and merchant stock on his father's."

On the other side of the room anxious eyes watched the absorbed couple. At length the Comtesse folded her fan.

"I don't like it, Justin, not du Plessis. 'Tis a pity you had to introduce him."

"You were the one who performed that office," responded her nephew.

"Well, I could hardly do otherwise, not when he was being so persistent, but surely you could warn him. . . ." She caught his expression and fell silent for a moment. "I thought you and he were friends."

"We were," came the cryptic response.

"No longer then?"

"I have a marked dislike of having my hand forced, Claudine!"

"Oh, you mean because he forced the introduction?"

"That among other things, although I fancy the introduction was scarcely necessary. That had already been effected."

The Marquis smiled rather grimly, and the Comtesse asked rather uneasily, "Justin, I trust it is no part of your plan to have *la petite* fall in love with du Plessis?"

It was a possibility that had not occurred to him, and that in itself was a little surprising. He found the notion oddly disturbing. "She will fall in love with her husband, and before you ask, that husband will not be du Plessis."

"He would be an excellent match."

"Claudine, you must be more of a romantic than I ever dreamed possible if you believe du Plessis entertains any notions of marriage!"

The Comtesse shrugged lightly. "You forget, Justin, you cannot order the child to fall in love at will. Besides, I do not understand. Why must she love her husband?"

"So that she will suffer the same pain as my mother."

"Justin, no! You cannot mean it?"

"But I do, Claudine," he told her savagely.

Chapter
6

There was a faint scratching at the door, and Louise de Liveaurac raised her aching head from lace-covered pillows to croak, *"Entres."*

She was a proud woman, but there was a limit to the length of time pride could keep hot tears at bay, and she had wept deep into the night. At first she had abandoned herself to a paroxysm of angry tears, and then lying dry-eyed, acknowledged the humiliating truth that she had overestimated her power over Saint-Vire, and because of that had lost not only her lover, but also possibly the position she had fought so long to gain. It wasn't easy for the daughter of minor and poor nobility to gain a foothold in Versailles, even one as beautiful as Louise, and now with one foolish action, she had thrown it all away. Had she even suspected for one moment that Saint-Vire would ignore her, she would never have tried to force him to introduce her to his ward. However, still smarting from the rebuff she had received in London, and unwilling to believe that he actually meant what he had said, she had gambled her all on her beauty—and had lost.

She shivered, recalling the contempt in his eyes, and the open amusement in other people's. She had lain on her bed in the darkness, admitting for the first time that she had lost him; indeed, had never really possessed him. The fever of love that had driven her for so many long weeks died, and she began to realize the price she had paid for his—his what? His desire? Certainly not his love; no woman had ever possessed that.

She waved away the maid hurrying into her room, summoned by the knocking on the door.

"Leave it, Jeanette, it will doubtless be Monsieur my brother."

It was. Monsieur Clary's face seemed more sallow than ever in the morning light, and it seemed impossible to believe that he was so closely related to the beautiful woman lying on the bed.

Coolly, he surveyed the evidence of the manner in which she had passed the night.

"You surprise me, sister. You can still weep for Saint-Vire, despite what he has done to you? Better you should weep for yourself. You realize he has made us the laughingstock of Versailles, and all for that wide-eyed chit? So the Marquis is too proud to present his ward to his mistress, is he? Well, he shall learn that pride can come very dear!"

His small eyes narrowed unpleasantly, hatred turning to distaste as they rested on the creamy expanse of shoulder and bosom exposed by the thin silk nightgown.

"Cover yourself, sister. I am not one of your lovers come a calling." Louise flushed at the contemptuous tone, but made no effort to do as he bid. Her brother was a cold fish, unmoved by the passions that stirred her blood.

"And if I do take lovers, who can blame me? Not you, the person who sold me to a man old enough to be my father just to get a court position." Thin color ran up under the yellow skin, but Jules Clary had not sought his sister out at this hour of the morning merely to quarrel with her. He contented himself with murmuring dryly, "Sold! Hardly that, my dear, and I did not notice you voicing any complaints at the time. You were glad enough to marry Armand even though he was an old man. After all, it did make you a Comtesse and give you the entree to Versailles."

"Very true, brother, but your reasons for arranging the match were hardly altruistic!"

He acknowledged her words with a cold smile.

"*Vraiment*, so we both benefited; I see no crime in that."

"As you have continued to benefit from my lovers?"

"All but Saint-Vire. It is a great pity you were so foolish, Louise. He was the richest prize of all, and you let him slip through your fingers."

Louise eyed her brother sulkily. What a man. Could he think of nothing but money?

"Saint-Vire would have given you nothing,

Jules. He is not the type who needs to pay for his *amours,* although I hardly expect you to understand that."

Jules Clary controlled his rising anger. It would avail him nothing to antagonize Louise and could do a great deal of harm. He shrugged.

"Well, I will allow my dear, that you probably know far more about that subject than I do."

Brother and sister stared at one another with mutual dislike.

"You are abroad early, Jules."

He ignored the curiosity, smiling coldly. It would be truer to say that he had never been to bed. He had never liked Saint-Vire with his cool arrogance and haughty pride, and even while Jules had been assessing the possible advantages of his sister's association with the man, his hatred had grown. Now there was nothing to keep it in check; it sprang from a bottomless well within him, deep and atavistic, directed not only at the man but also at everything he stood for: privilege, rank, and wealth. Jules had known right from the start that Saint-Vire would never accept his challenge, but it gave him the excuse he needed. It had not been easy to find the men he wanted in the filthy warrens of the *cours des miracles;* those stinking alleys and crumbling mud huts that comprised the thieves' kitchens of Paris, where any villainy could be had—for a price—and what he wanted had come dear. However, he had at length been successful, and before too long Saint-Vire would learn what it meant to insult a Clary. The vermin of Paris were no respectors of name or title.

They owned only one god—money—and with that one could buy their very souls.

Louise slid from the bed, pulling on a wrapper and pacing the floor, the silk hissing angrily across the parquet.

"*Dieu*, Jules, I am not such a fool as you think. If I had even for one moment suspected that he would cut me I would never . . ." She swung around, hectic color spots in both cheeks. "How could he, Jules? I thought he cared a little for me at least, but to do that." Unconsciously she echoed Georgianna's words. "He must have known it would ruin me."

"Us, sister," corrected Jules, "and as for caring for you, if you ever believed that, you are worse than a fool. Saint-Vire cares for no one but himself. You handled the matter badly all along. You should have played on his desire for you, fanned it, not thrown yourself at him like some stupid country innocent."

"Careful, brother, else you will work yourself up into an apoplexy."

Controlling his temper with effort, he agreed. "You are right, Loise, this is no time for us to be quarreling."

"No? Then what brings you here, Jules? Brotherly love? I think not."

Jules Clary watched her shrewdly. He knew her better than she knew herself, and he was well aware of the inward battle, little though he was able to understand it. Desire for the love of another human being was a completely foreign emotion to Monsieur Clary, and in his opinion a time-consuming and futile one.

"On the contrary, Louise. After all, you are

my sister, and you have suffered an unpardonable insult. Indeed, I think it best that we retire from Versailles for a while. No doubt next week there will be some fresh scandal to keep the tongues clacking."

Louise stopped her pacing, dismayed.

"Retire from Versailles! Are you completely mad, Jules? A fine brother you are. I am insulted, thrown aside like a rag doll, scorned, and defiled, and all you can do is say we must run away. You are a poor apology for a man," she sneered. "Even Armand, old though he was . . ."

"Enough!" The word was a cold command.

"I am not running away; rather call it a tactical withdrawal if you must give it a name. Believe me, Louise, Saint-Vire will rue the day he insulted you."

She turned a startled and uneasy face in his direction. "*Dieu*, Jules, be careful," she warned. "Tell me, what have you done?"

"Done? Why, nothing, Louise, Nothing at all. Now come, call your maid. We leave this morning."

He turned on his heel and she was alone. There were times when she was almost frightened of her brother. She shuddered. If he should try to harm Saint-Vire. Uneasily she started to cross the room. No, surely he would not be so foolish; to harm a member of the nobility meant a long and protracted death. A fresh shudder wracked her.

In the Bois, the marquis gave his mount its head. Normally he enjoyed this part of the day, riding through the quiet woods while the rest of the world slept. The breeze was cool against his skin, blowing away the staleness of the previous evening and making him feel alive, but this morning he had too much on his mind.

He had been quite honest when he had told his aunt that it was no part of his aim to see his ward fall in love with Philippe du Plessis, or any other gentleman of his ilk; had that been the case the easiest thing in the world would have been to make her fall in love with himself. He made the admission without vanity, too familiar with the feminine sex to doubt that it would have been possible. Would? Did he then think that it was no longer possible? He shrugged the thought aside; it was merely academic.

Philippe du Plessis would no more contemplate marrying a girl like Georgianna than he would himself, and the Marquis was not prepared to sit back and allow his ward to make sheep's eyes at one of France's most notorious rakes. Only by seeing his ward embark on a long and unhappy marriage could he savor the full measure of his revenge. He recalled the two fair heads so close together the previous evening. And the guilty manner in which Georgianna had sprung away from du Plessis, when she had seen him bearing down upon them. If she thought he would stand by and allow her to indulge in idle flirtation with Philippe du Plessis, she would soon learn her mistake. And as for du Plessis himself! His mouth tightened repressively.

Engrossed in these thoughts, he did not notice the slight movement in the thicket ahead of him, and he rode on unaware of the danger lurking there.

Georgianna, too, had awoken early. Sleep had been a long time in coming and had then been filled with uneasy dreams. She recalled guiltily the look on Saint-Vire's face when he had come across her in a small alcove, deep in conversation with Philippe.

The look Saint-Vire had given her had spoken quite clearly of retribution to come. Uneasily she recalled other details of the evening; her own refusal to speak to him, and the Comtesse's unhappy face. She reached for the bell. She would have to apologize, and the sooner she got it over the better. Then she remembered. Saint-Vire went riding in the morning.

Warm sunshine poured through a chink in the curtains; in the closet hung the charming riding habits that had been bought for her, as yet neither of them worn. Perhaps a brisk ride would put her in a more dutiful frame of mind.

Half an hour later found her descending the stairs. Jacques, hovering in the hallway, bowed gravely.

"I thought I would ride with my guardian," supplied Georgianna unnecessarily. "Has he been gone very long, Jacques?"

She fiddled a little nervously with her gloves, hoping the man would not think her request too strange. Her relief was quite apparent when after a few moments' thought he offered gravely,

"Only a few minutes, M'mselle. I'm sure you will be able to catch up with him."

Feeling a need to allay something of her fear, Georgianna confided, "I'm afraid I might have made him a little angry."

She peeped up at the wooden countenance, while Jacques, always the gentleman, reassured her: "Monsieur le Comte was just as usual, M'mselle."

Jacques watched her go with a sympathetic grimace. So far his experiences of his master's temper did not lead him to place too much reliance on the success of Georgianna's mission.

The morning was crisp. There was the faintest touch of frost on the smooth, green-velvet turf, the ride widening out invitingly as Georgianna trotted sedately in her guardian's wake. It should not take her too long to catch up with him, and yet perversely she allowed her mount to dawdle, the coming interview lying heavily on her mind.

Fair-mindedly she allowed that after all he had only been doing his duty, yet she could not forget the woman's stricken face, or the titters that had followed her departure. And then there had been the matter of Philippe. Georgianna sighed. She liked Philippe; he was fun, making her laugh with his ridiculous compliments, teasing her gently, and in no way behaving in a rakish manner. He was far nicer than her guardian, and she would have him for her friend whatever Saint-Vire said. This decision made, she allowed her mount its head. The morning was far too lovely to waste on introspection. Her guardian, her apology, and her conscience could all wait while she savored the freshness of the morning.

Sunlight dappled through the trees, casting faint moving shadows as the breeze stirred the fresh young leaves; her mount shied at the sudden emergence of an inquisitive squirrel that chattered crossly at them, shaking the branches with its anger. A streak of sunlight silvered Georgianna's hair, startling against the rich depths of the blue velvet, cut by a master hand to enhance the slender lines of her figure. It was hard to be unhappy when everything about her sang of joy and life. Her lips parted in a smile. Surely on a morning like this there could be no strife. The thought brought a rueful twinkle to her eyes. Her guardian, instinct told her, was no respecter of lovely mornings. Doubtless he would soon shatter the peace with his harsh words and cold looks.

Then Georgianna remembered his mother. Poor boy, he must have been terribly lonely when she had gone. She only had to think of her own childhood—and she had never really known her mother. Although it had never been referred to since, she had been unable to forget the sad little tale his aunt had told her. She no longer believed that it was "kindness" that had prompted the Marquis to bring her to Paris. This thought saddened her, because she knew there could never be that close relationship between them she had once hoped for; she could not be wholly sorry, however, for after all, had it not brought her to the Comtesse, whose love warmed her like summer sun, and Philippe, whom she already . . . Georgianna started. Surely she was not going to fall in love with Philippe? He liked her, that she knew, and once or twice she had surprised a gleam in his eyes that had made her feel vaguely breathless. Common sense told her that to fall in love with Philippe du Plessis was to court danger. The thought of love brought her mind back to her guardian.

The Comtesse, and a little less delicately Conde too, had hinted that many women did love him. Georgianna shivered. He would not be an easy man to love; that cold, distant manner would always be a barrier, or was there perhaps another side to him that she had not been privileged to see? A warmer side, where the gray eyes grew tender, and the hard mouth softened. The thought disturbed her. Of course, he was very handsome, no one could deny that, and quite obviously his mistress must have loved him very much. Georgianna blushed guiltily, thankful that there was no one to see her embarrassment. Had she seen a different face from the one he showed the world? Surely she must have done. Surely there must be a more pliant strain to his nature, which was only revealed by the lover? Georgianna recalled the hardness of his fingers gripping her arm.

To be held in his arms would be like being imprisoned with iron bars. Aware that her thoughts were less than modest, she blushed afresh, blaming the beauty of the morning, and urging her horse forward. A brisk canter would clear her mind. The animal, fresh from the stable, leaped forward at her touch, and they were flying over the ground, the wind tearing through her hair. The groom, insisted upon by the Marquis' coachman, was left far behind. After the first few seconds Georgianna made no attempt to check her mount, instead reveling in the sudden sensation of speed and freedom. By the time the horse had run off its energy they were in a small glade, bordered by a clump of trees. Before her etched on the horizon, she saw the figure of the man she had come to find.

Her heart thumped uncomfortably. Now that the moment was upon her, she wished that she had waited at the hotel and allowed him to seek her out.

Just as she was about to call out to him, there was a faint sound, like a twig snapping— and yet somehow different—which reverberated through the silence of the morning, shattering the peace, and then died away, leaving an unnerving silence. Some dim prescience of danger kept her still, and then to her consternation Georgianna saw the Marquis slowly slump in the saddle, lingering for a moment over the horse's neck, before falling to the ground.

She swallowed hard, suddenly recognizing the sound for what it had been. A pistol. Someone had shot her guardian. The fear that had held her motionless went, driven out by anxiety for the man lying on the ground.

Soon, she and her horse were thundering over the ground with reckless disregard for rabbit-holes and any lurking thieves.

Ignoring the possible consequences to her expensive habit, Georgianna slid from the saddle. Her guardian was quite motionless. Anxiously she bent over the inert figure. There was a gash on the white forehead, a thin trickle of blood matting the dark hair.

"Monsieur?" Her voice trembled.

The man never moved. His face was as white as the lace at his neck, wiped clean of all expression, the mouth no longer twisted or mocking, dark lashes concealing his eyes. Horrified, Georgianna sank down at his side, her velvet billowing out around her. Gently she took his head in her lap, dabbing frantically at the wound with her handkerchief. Why didn't someone come? Anxiously she scanned the clearing; nothing moved, no welcome sound of horses' hooves broke the stillness of the morning. She did not even know if he still lived! Tentatively she touched his face, and then, her eyes never leaving his face, reached inside his coat to lay trembling fingers on the wellspring of human life. Unbelievably she could feel the reassuring thud of his heart, steady beneath her hand. For a moment she was too dazed with relief to move. She let her hand lie where it was, against the comforting rise and fall of his chest. Who had shot him? Thieves probably. Paris abounded with them, or so the Comtesse had said, living in those dreadful places they called the *cours des miracles*, preying on the unwary. She shivered again. What if they were to come back? What chance would a wounded man and a defenseless girl have? For the Marquis it would mean death—but for her? Desperately Georgianna prayed. If only her groom would come. Even now someone might be watching them from the safety of those bushes, watching and waiting. . . . But she knew she could not leave him.

She touched the wound with gentle fingers, smoothing back the thick dark hair; it felt soft and silky. Deep down inside she trembled; the thick lashes lifted and she found herself staring straight into the familiar gray eyes.

He lifted his head from her lap, wincing a little. "Georgianna, what . . . ?"

Hastily she intervened, glad of something to hide her confusion. "Someone shot at you."

He fingered the wound tentatively. "And missed me, by the looks of it. Did you see them?"

Slowly Georgianna shook her head. She had expected him to betray more concern than he was doing. "I thought it must be thieves." She shivered again. "I kept thinking they might still be here."

"And yet you stayed with me?" His eyes held hers.

"I could not leave a wounded man."

"Very pretty," he sneered. "I suppose it didn't occur to you that I might die, leaving you as my ward a very rich heiress?"

Georgianna couldn't believe she had heard aright. "I care nothing for your fortune."

"No? You are already thinking of Philippe's, perhaps. I would not be too optimistic if I were you. Philippe du Plessis is very skilled at avoiding the matrimonial net."

Georgianna gasped. He could not honestly believe she thought Philippe would want to marry her. Why, they had only just met, and besides, hadn't he, himself, told her that he would not? Her initial relief at his safety was rapidly turning to rage at his accusations.

"Philippe is a friend, nothing more."

"Indeed," he jeered. "Tell me, are your friendships always conducted with such fervor, or is Philippe du Plessis particularly favored?"

Georgianna knew without him saying that he referred to the previous evening, when he had found them together, one of the very things she had come to apologize for.

"You don't want me to care for anyone," she flung at him. "You want me to be like you, cold and distant; well, I won't."

There was an unnerving silence.

"Cold, distant! So not content with wanting to call me 'uncle' and saddling me with a ready-made family, you now intend to define my character as well. And you, of course, have much experience!"

Georgianna could hardly believe it. Nervously she looked around. If only her groom had come. It must have been the blow to his head. Never had she seen him so uncontrolled. She was used to his biting sarcasm, but not this. Dimly she sensed that her words had unleashed something inside him, something all the more dangerous simply because it was normally held rigorously in check.

He was breathing heavily, his eyes glittering as they raked her pale face. "Well, miss, allow me to add experience to your inventiveness."

Scarcely had she comprehended the words, than she was seized in a hard embrace. Recalling her earlier thoughts she trembled; his arms were like iron. They held her fiercely against his chest, so that its warmth seemed to burn through her habit and into her own skin.

"Let me go!"

It was the cry of a frightened child, but he seemed unable to hear it. His mouth came down on hers, bruising, forceful, totally different from the kisses of her imagination. Her last thought was, Philippe would not kiss me like this, and then there was only outrage for what she sensed to be a gross insult. There was nothing gentle in the pressure of his mouth on hers, nothing tender or warm. Surely no woman would want to be embraced like this?

When he let her go he was breathing hard; his face was white and strained, and there was a blank look about his eyes.

"Well, do you still find me cold?"

Dearly as she would have liked to argue the point, Georgianna had not the strength. She felt shocked and drained, her sensibilities bruised. Never had she imagined him behaving in such a fashion. She almost felt she hated him. She drew as far away from him as possible.

"I followed you this morning to apologize for my conduct last night, but now . . ." She turned away in distress, wondering at the muscle that twitched faintly in the hard jawline. All her restraint deserted her. The shock of seeing him shot, and then the horror that had followed. "You are hateful, hateful," she flung at him. "Worse than my father. He was content to ignore me, but that is not enough for you, you have to insult me as well. I wish I had never met you."

In that moment she was a very hurt child, wounded by the behavior of adults whom she could not understand.

Somehow, she mounted her horse and turned its head in the direction she had come, her mind a jangling cacophony of sensation. That dreadful kiss. Again she shuddered.

It wasn't until she regained the sanctuary of her room that she realized her apology had never been made. Nor ever would be, now she told herself. How could she endure to spend another day in the same house as her guardian? He must hate her to have treated her so. No more than I hate him, she told herself fiercely. And this was the man she had wanted to love and revere. She threw herself down on the bed and gave way to hysterical laughter.

It might have lessened Georgianna's anger had she known she was not the only one to be shocked.

Monsieur le Comte de Saint-Vire was not in the habit of indulging in such uncontrolled behavior; indeed, he was renowned for his *savoir faire*. He watched his ward ride away with hard eyes. Doubtless she would take refuge in the arms of Philippe du Plessis. Not normally a man to doubt his own ability, it occurred to him that his plans were going somewhat awry. He touched the wound on his scalp. Another inch and he would still be lying on the ground, dead. His mouth hardened again. That stupid child.

Didn't she know the risks she ran in staying with him? His attackers could have returned at any moment, and a girl like Georgianna would fetch a good price in any one of the brothels that abounded in Paris. Something—shame? regret?—moved him uncomfortably. He ignored it. It was no noble instinct that had prompted her to stay with him, just ignorance of her real danger.

And now . . . he turned toward Paris. He was nearly clear of the Bois when the sound of horses' hooves and the rattle of wheels heralded the arrival of a carriage. As it came into view, he stared at it, his expression suddenly menacing. It was a carriage remarkable only by its shabbiness and the poor quality of the horseflesh that drew it. Surely there could be no reason for it to excite his attention, and yet nevertheless he seemed curiously interested in it.

He stood by the roadside and waited. The carriage drew abreast of him, and the driver had perforce to stop, as he was blocking the road. Dismounting, he sauntered to the door.

"*Eh bien,* Monsieur Clary, and leaving Paris, unless I am mistaken. I trust not as a result of our small *contretemps* last night?"

Jules Clary shrank back against the hard seat, his body shaking as though with the ague. Small drops of perspiration beaded his forehead and upper lip, and a smile ghastly to behold stretched his mouth. One strangled word was torn from his lips:

"You!"

"As you so rightly say," drawled the Marquis. "Fate it seems is not disposed to be kind to you, Monsieur. I appear to have given you something of a shock. My appearance, I doubt not. You must excuse it. I had the misfortune to sustain a slight accident this morning." He said no more, but it was enough.

Louise de Liveaurac stared from her brother to the Marquis. She had been right: Jules had planned something, and failed! It was enough to glance at her brother to see his fear.

Jules Clary was more than frightened. He was terrified, possessed by the superstitious dread of a man who sees an enemy risen from the dead.

"You seem in something of a hurry," drawled the hated voice. "Indeed, one would almost be forgiven for thinking the Devil himself were at your heels." The simile was unpleasantly apt.

Jules Clary laughed harshly. "Your imagination runs away with you, Saint-Vire. Nothing so alarming, merely a sick relative. We go to his bedside."

"Oh." The Marquis surveyed the ruby adorning one long finger.

"Then your absence is merely of a temporary nature?"

Clary congratulated himself. The excuse of a sick relative was a good one, but the imaginery malaise was nothing to what those two bunglers would experience when he got his hands on them, he thought viciously.

Without waiting for an answer, the Marquis continued blandly, "Well I must not detain you, it would be a pity if you were to arrive too late." There was a slight pause. "I shall look forward to seeing you when you return to Versailles. You will not disappoint me, I hope?"

Monsieur Clary recovered sufficiently to remark unpleasantly, "We shall be there, Saint-Vire, but I doubt you will be able to tear yourself away from your ward long enough to see us." He paused significantly. "Tell me, do you and du Plessis intend to share her favors between you? It will be quite like old times I . . ."

He got no farther. Long fingers curled around his throat, jerking him out of his seat.

"I should be very careful if I were you, Clary."

"I only repeat what they are already whispering in Versailles," he defended.

"Nevertheless I should be careful; life is a chancy thing at best."

"You have had your chance to kill me and you refused to take it."

"My dear Clary, you mistake. I was but expressing concern for your welfare. These woods abound with thieves and cutthroats, as I myself have occasion to know." Gently he released the man. "By the way, Clary, I should be displeased if I were to hear the name of my ward on your lips again. You understand?" The Marquis stepped back and motioned to the postillions to drive on.

Chapter
7

In the days that followed Georgianna's presentation, and that all too intrusive moment in the woods, the Marquis' tall figure became a familiar sight in his old haunts, the famous salons, and some of the less reputable houses. However, he never seemed to stay long. He would arrive late, glance around with cynical eyes and a thin smile, and generally leave after no more than the briefest stay. His expression would be withdrawn as he glanced over the gaming tables, or exchanged pleasantries with an old acquaintance. Such behavior could hardly pass unnoticed, and gradually the whispers grew. Saint-Vire, it was rumored, had become a reformed character. He had always been a remote figure, held in awe by his contemporaries, but never more so than now. Tongues wagged; old scandals were raked up, and people wondered. Everyone knew he had cast off his mistress and yet had found no one to replace her. Then there was his charming ward—a piquant situation if you liked. Paris watched and waited.

Neither had Philippe been idle. Hardly a

day passed without him sending Georgianna some expensive trifle designed to charm any young lady. Fans, baskets of fruit, and often Philippe himself. Indeed, so frequently did he visit the Hotel Saint-Vire that the Marquis was heard to drawl savagely that he could not step inside his home without falling over the gentleman, a remark that occasioned a raised eyebrow from his aunt. The Comtesse was rapidly revising her opinion of the young man. Nothing could be more convenable than his behavior toward Georgianna. To see him with her, so attentive, so protective, was quite charming, and the Comtesse ventured to say as much to her nephew. Saint-Vire, however, was not disposed to be charmed, and gave his aunt to understand that the popular fiction that reformed rakes make the best husbands was no more than just that. The Comtesse kept her own council, and seeing her nephew's brooding look refrained from hazarding the guess that she would see her charge a Comtesse yet.

It seemed she was to be proved right. Rising late one night from the tables after a particularly good run of luck, the Marquis found his way barred by Armand du Plessis, Philippe's uncle. This circumstance was surprising enough in itself to cause comment, for Armand was that rarity among the nobility of France, a man of unassailable morality.

The Marquis reached for his snuff box, his expression veiled. "Why, Armand, you here?"

Armand's glance encompassed the room and its other occupants in a manner that was not lost on that gentleman. He pursed small, almost feminine lips, and rocked back on his heels, hands folded piously over his ample stomach. "Duty brings me here, Saint-Vire."

"Duty, you don't say. How very laudable," commended the Marquis. "You are, perhaps, searching for converts?"

Muffled laughter greeted this sally, for Armand's propensity for lecturing on the sadly depraved morals of his fellows was well known.

"It is you I wished to see, Saint-Vire," responded du Plessis stiffly.

"Ah, I see, you are not searching for converts. Nevertheless I am flattered, Armand. Your business must indeed be urgent if it makes you seek me out here."

Du Plessis glanced around, his distaste only thinly disguised. "I own to not have a taste for such things. I would not willingly spend my time here. I came, however, to talk to you over the matter of my nephew."

The Marquis glanced reflectively at his companion, his voice dropping to a dulcet murmur. "I think this matter could best be discussed in the privacy of my hotel."

Flushing under the rebuke, du Plessis retorted, "Certainement. If one was able to find you there, but the matter becomes urgent, Saint-Vire. It is being whispered all over Paris that young Philippe and this ward of yours are to make a match of it."

"I see. And Philippe sends you to tell me otherwise?" Scorn thinned his voice.

Too surprised to be wary, du Plessis stared

at him. "What? No, you have it all wrong. I dare swear he would take the chit dowryless, he's so mad for her."

There was an ominous glint in the gray eyes now, and a dinstinctly tense atmosphere about his person. "I confess, du Plessis, I do not care for the thought that all Paris gossips about my ward."

Before he could continue, Conde wandered into the room and saw them. "Armand, you here? I thought you disapproved?"

That unhappy gentleman, torn between a desire to express his disapproval in no uncertain terms and at the same time acknowledge the respect due to royalty, remarked rather disjointedly that business had brought him.

"I wanted to see Saint-Vire."

Conde shot the Marquis an amused glance. "Did you so? To beg an introduction to his so-charming ward, I doubt not." Theatrically he placed one hand over his heart. "Ah, we are all a little *epris* in that direction, *mon ami*, but if you think Saint-Vire will look kindly on your suit, forget it. He has become a veritable paragon of virtue."

Du Plessis stared at him suspiciously, coming to the reluctant conclusion that royal blood or not, there was an unbecoming degree of levity in the young man's behavior.

The Marquis favored him with a cool smile. "Fascinating though our discussion was, du Plessis, I think it can best be continued at a later date."

Faced with this dismissal, the unfortunate de Plessis had to take his leave.

Conde turned to the Marquis, brown eyes dancing. "A pity our respectable Armand is also so boringly dull, Saint-Vire. What did he want?" He did not wait for a reply. "Tell me, Saint-Vire, what think you of this?" From his pocket he withdrew a fan, spreading it laughingly for his inspection. "Amusing, is it not? It is a gift from La Fontaine in Italy."

"A pretty trifle," agreed the Marquis, studying the gold design picked out on the black background. "The nymphs are perhaps a little on the Junoesque?"

"Yes," agreed Conde, "but therein lies its charm. With a deft flick of his wrist Conde held the fan before his face: "*Voilà*, I am outraged." He closed it with a snap, unfurling it again, on a languorous sigh and fluttering it before his eyes. "*Eh bien*, now I am *ennuyee*, yes?"

The Marquis grinned. "You are ridiculous, yes!"

"Ridiculous! Saint-Vire, how can you? They are all the rage. I give you my word. What did Armand want?"

Despite the dexterous manner in which he slipped the question in, a mocking glance told him that his companion was not deceived.

"He wanted to tell me that Paris is aflame with gossip concerning my ward and Philippe."

Conde noted the twisted smile and remarked casually, "Yes, amusing, it is not, our Philippe a victim of cupid's dart."

"You will forgive me, Conde, but I, for one, cannot find the spectacle of my ward casting sheep's eyes at a rake like du Plessis particularly edifying."

"Sheep's eyes—that charming child! Surely not? But come, Saint-Vire, you make too much of it, and besides, I believe on this occasion it is Philippe who is the victim."

The Marquis, with his back to the doorway, unlike Conde, did not have the benefit of seeing Philippe enter the room, and Conde's mischievous Devil always on the alert prompted him now to say nothing of the other's presence to his companion.

Thus it was that Philippe du Plessis was at his elbow before Saint-Vire was aware of his presence.

"Saint-Vire. Conde."

The Marquis' response was far from warm, and so was the look he threw Conde. "Well, du Plessis, quite a family gathering. First your good uncle and now you."

"Armand was here?"

Conde laughed. "Oh indeed. Bent on a mission of great importance." Idly he unfurled the fan again. "Apparently he fears for your virtue, Philippe, at the hands of Saint-Vire's ward, no less." The fan stilled.

Philippe looked from Conde's laughing face to Saint-Vire's set one. "Saint-Vire?"

In the tension-filled silence their glances met and locked, but when the Marquis did speak it was in his normal cool drawl. "You can hardly suppose me to relish hearing my ward's name coupled with yours, du Plessis."

Philippe eyed him quizzically. "You make too much of it, my friend. You cannot suppose I would dishonor *la petite*," he offered laughingly. His laughter was suddenly stilled by what

144

he read in the other's eyes. "*Dieu!*" he swore softly. "Or is it that I mistake the matter and you can!" He then spoke so softly that only Conde and the Marquis caught his words: "If so, you impugn not only my honor, but Miss Lawley's as well, and that. . . . offends me . . . Saint-Vire."

Conde's sharp eyes noticed the significant manner in which his hand dropped to his sword hilt, and the blazing anger in the blue eyes, and then the moment was gone. Whatever else he might not be Philippe du Plessis was a gentleman, and a lady's honor was not the subject for a public brawl. The blue eyes were laughing again.

"Well, Conde, what think you? How does this new role suit our friend here? You find him a good guardian, *non?* I vow he looks as though he would run me through for a handful of ecus. Justin, I despair, what has happened to my old companion?" He shook his head. "You really should be grateful to me, Saint-Vire. After all, without me to distract her, your lovely ward might fall in love with you. A sad waste, don't you agree? The enchanting Georgianna languishing for your smile, and you having to enact the stern guardian. I vow it would be an amusing sight."

"Not half as amusing as the sight of my sword sticking through your heart, Philippe, I assure you," ground out his victim.

Philippe grinned and bowed low. "Tomorrow, Saint-Vire, I have the pleasure of escorting your ward to the Bois on a picnic, with Madame la Comtesse, of course."

The gray eyes were faintly shadowed. "Have you now, Philippe; a picnic, you say. How delightful."

"Indeed, Saint-Vire. I am quite sure it will be. And now, gentlemen, good night."

Conde laughed again as they watched him go, suddenly becoming serious. "He is right, Justin, you are taking your responsibilities over seriously."

"You think I should allow him to seduce the girl unhindered, is that it?"

"Seduce, Saint-Vire? You cannot be serious. Why, it is all over Paris that du Plessis will offer for the girl. Can you doubt it?"

"You think so? What about la Francine's daughter?" Conde shrugged callously. "The girl was already secondhand goods. *La petite* is different. Can it be that you do not want him to marry her?" He smiled wickedly. "Perhaps you are a little *epris* yourself?"

The look he received would have annihilated another man. "I trust you are but jesting, Conde?"

Conde eyed him kindly.

"You are becoming something unapproachable over this matter of your ward, Justin. Be careful, I beg you."

With this cryptic utterance he took his leave, and it was left to Georgianna to bear the full brunt of his temper the next morning when she was summoned to his presence shortly after breakfast.

The morning in the Bois and its unforgettable conclusion lay between them like a deep, silent pool, unmentioned and yet acknowledged. Warily Georgianna skirted the room, standing as far from him as possible. Sunlight glinted, dancing off the silvery curls, touching one cheek, as soft and tempting as any peach, and yet the Marquis appeared quite unmoved by his ward's undeniable beauty. She was wearing a demure morning gown of palest pink, embellished with lace flounces and knots of ribbons. Her guardian was looking as immaculate as he always did and had obviously changed his riding clothes for more formal attire.

"Ah, my charming ward."

Something in his voice alerted her. Instinctively she stiffened, and the action only seemed to goad him further.

"Such maidenly cringing, scarcely necessary, I would have thought. I am not Philippe du Plessis."

Georgianna opened her mouth to announce tartly that she had never for one moment supposed he was—there was no need for her to cringe away from Philippe. He did not . . . A fiery blush suffused her cheeks. That was a subject better not touched upon. If her guardian could forget that it had ever taken place, then so most certainly could she. She swallowed hard on her anger. "You wanted to see me?"

"Indeed I did."

They were in the library, the gold curtains billowing out a little in the breeze. Georgianna fixed her eyes on the open windows, trying to quell the increasingly unpleasant flutterings in the region of her stomach.

The Marquis seated himself behind his

desk, leaning forward, his elbows on the leather surface, the tips of his fingers together. "It has come to my ears, Georgianna, that your name is constantly being coupled with du Plessis."

Georgianna shrugged. "We are together a good deal, I suppose. . . ."

"You do not find it unpleasant then that your virtue, or loss of it, is the talk of Paris?"

Hot color flooded Georgianna's face. Anger, so intense that it practically choked her, boiled up inside her, but still the sneering voice continued. "I seem to remember not so very long ago warning you against du Plessis. Tell me, do you deliberately disregard what I tell you, or is it mere chance?"

Georgianna tossed her head airily. She would not be browbeaten by him, and neither would she allow him to frighten her.

"I like Philippe. . ."

"Despite the fact that he is renowned for his *amours,* and that everyone already believes you are halfway to becoming his mistress."

"That is not true." The words were out before she could prevent them, and seeing the steely glint with which she was being regarded, she had no choice but to continue. "How can you of all people sit there and say that about Philippe? He has been all that is gentlemanly." Seeing that he was still regarding her with weary cynicism, she added defiantly, "At least he doesn't kiss me against my will." Appalled, Georgianna cursed her runaway tongue.

On the other side of the desk the Marquis

never moved, and yet Georgianna had the impression that if he could, he would have taken her by the throat and shaken her until she dropped.

In a voice silky with venom he asked her, "And what exactly does that mean? That he doesn't kiss you, or that his kisses aren't unwanted?"

His eyes told her quite plainly that he knew the answer.

Across the table they challenged one another. Blue eyes hot and gray eyes cold. There was something indefinable in the air. A challenge that had nothing to do with Philippe. Now all pretense of good manners or duty was stripped from them. They were antagonists.

It was the Marquis who broke the silence. "Don't think Philippe will marry you. He won't. He will use you for as long as you suit his purpose, and then you will be case aside."

Quietly, her head held proudly, Georgianna told him, "I am not Philippe's mistress, nor do I intend to become one. But even if I were, I do not believe he would treat me like that. He is not like you."

The words hung between them.

Georgianna's face turned toward the desk, dismayed by what she saw. The Marquis's face was white, even his lips seemed drained of blood, and in contrast his eyes blazed furiously.

"Georgianna! Justin!"

It took the Comtesse's appalled cry to break the spell that bound them together.

With a small cry Georgianna whirled from the room.

"Lud, Justin, what were you about?"

"Merely trying to warn my ward," he emphasized the last word heavily, "not to place too much importance on Philippe du Plessis's attentions."

"Really; then I think your warnings are unnecessary," was the crisp retort. "You are too hard on the child, Justin. I have told you before, things are not always what they seem. In her way she has suffered just as much as you. Let her have what happiness she can."

"Even if it means finding it in the arms of du Plessis?"

"He is a man, like any other, and he loves her."

"And you think that is enough?"

Wearily the Marquis got to his feet and left.

The result of the altercation with her guardian was a headache that kept Georgianna in bed until she heard Philippe's voice floating through her window. Of course the picnic. The picnic was originally the Comtesse's idea, for she fancied Georgianna's cheeks had grown a little pale of late and had decided that such an outing would do her charge good. She was unaware that the blame for this could more properly be laid at the feet of her nephew rather than a lack of fresh air. Georgianna was none too happy with the suggestion. The woods did not hold happy memories for her. And yet, often when she was alone, she found herself dwelling on the incident, a funny little pain twisting her heart, yearning for something only dimly imagined. She felt she had come a long way from the girl who had stood in the dusty roadway and admired the Marquis. How could she ever have been foolish enough to suppose that such a man would feel any fondness for her?

By the time she had bathed her eyes and brushed her curls, the rest of the party was assembled downstairs. Originally it was to have comprised Philippe, the Comtesse, and herself, but now had swelled to include the Marquis and a cousin of Philippe's.

Georgianna arrived downstairs just in time for the introductions, and wondered if she could have imagined the strange look she saw exchanged by the Marquis and Philippe. Philippe, bowing over her hand and squeezing her fingers gently, made his cousin known to her. "Georgianna, my cousin, Madame la Marquesse de Grand-Sauval."

A gentle hand raised her from her curtsy, a warm, laughing voice whispering in her ear. "Georgianna, how delightful. You must call me Anne."

"Saint-Vire, you of course already know my cousin, although you may have forgotten her. She has been away from Paris for many years."

Again that look between them!

Courteously he bowed over the lady's hand. Georgianna had never seen her guardian behaving in the grand manner before. There was no doubt that he was exceedingly accomplished.

With grave formality he released the lady's hand. "Madame, of course I remember you. Who could forget such beauty?"

Georgianna was amazed. She just caught Philippe's whispered "I shall explain all later," before the Comtesse was urging them all toward the door.

A strange feeling of desolation swept over Georgianna as she saw the Marquis place Anne's fingers on his arm; the smile he gave her was warm, chasing away the bitterness she was so used to seeing.

Anne smiled up at him. A warm, entrancing gesture, wholly without conceit. The Marquis' other hand touched her arm, as though they were enveloped in a private world of their own from which everyone else was excluded. Then Philippe was at Georgianna's side. They were in the carriage and on their way.

If anything, the woods were lovelier now than they had been on that fateful morning. They traversed leafy avenues, cool green tunnels, here and there a patch of deep blue, where bluebells still flowered, mingling with the scarlet of early poppies. Philippe drew her attention to a small pond and its occupants, a large, placid mother duck and her brood. It seemed impossible to believe that death could lurk unseen in this green paradise.

Georgianna shivered.

"Surely you aren't cold?" The Comtesse was instantly concerned. Anne's lovely profile turned toward her, the blue eyes, so very like her cousin's, expressing sympathy.

"No," said Georgianna. "I was just hoping there wouldn't be any thieves."

"Thieves! My dear child, there would not be nowadays. Once yes, but now you will find them in Paris, not here, isn't that so?" appealed the Comtesse.

Only the Marquis remained silent in the chorus of voices agreeing with the Comtesse's pronouncement.

Anne's silvery voice commiserated with her. "I know what you mean, Georgianna. It would be frightening to be lost here alone."

Georgianna was stunned at the tender expression she surprised on her guardian's face. How he must love her! So he was capable of love then! And yet he hates me! She bit her lip, unaware that her hands were tightly clenched in her lap.

The small glade was everything Philippe had promised them it would be. A small stream gurgled through the shade of the trees; grassy banks invited the eye. Georgianna felt the tranquillity of the spot reach out and enfold her. She turned to address her guardian, but he was totally absorbed in assisting Anne to alight from the carriage. She sighed unconsciously. The picnic itself was a very grand affair. Tasty pasties, a selection of cold viands, jellies, and dainty trifles to tempt the appetite of the most fastidious lady, and cool, refreshing wine. No wonder that the Comtesse reposed herself for a small sleep.

Half warily, Georgianna glanced at her guardian, but he seemed totally engrossed in his conversation with Anne. All through the picnic the two had talked. Not as strangers do, but as old friends, in low voices, totally lost in reminiscences, punctuated here and there by Anne's trilling laugh, and to Georgianna's surprise, the deeper one of Saint-Vire. The man revealed to her by Anne's softening presence was a stranger, and she felt a twinge of regret that it had been left to Anne to show her this other side to her guardian.

The Marquis was lying on his back, careless of his velvet, with his eyes closed. Anne was sitting at his side, talking quickly, now and then glancing down into his face, as though awaiting his response. They were so close that her gown billowed over him. Georgianna's heart ached for something lost and yet never really known.

Philippe led her from the glade, down a narrow path to where the stream fed a pool. The stillness of the afternoon lay all around them like a golden haze. Fish jumped lazily, falling back into the water with a soft splash. Gently Philippe pulled her down to sit beside him. "You like my cousin?"

"Who could not? She is charming, but a little sad."

"You noticed that, did you. Poor Anne, she has had much to endure."

Georgianna raked the grass with her fingers.

"She and my guardian seem to know one another well."

"Yes. She came to Versailles not long after Saint-Vire arrived in France. I was there myself. Everyone adored her."

"I'm not surprised. She is very lovely."

Philippe laughed softly. "But not as lovely as you." He leaned toward her, and instinctively Georgianna jerked away. Saint-Vire's embrace was still far too fresh in her mind for her to want any others. Philippe did not seem to notice. He touched her cheek gently. "Now, where was I? Ah yes, I was telling you about Anne and Saint-Vire, wasn't I? They became close friends. Anne is only a year younger than I."

A small frown creased Georgianna's brow. "You mean they were in love?"

Philippe shrugged. "*Certainement*, or so it seemed, but Anne was promised already. An excellent match."

"Oh, and they had to part. How sad."

It seemed her guardian had had a lot of unhappiness in his life.

Philippe smiled lazily. "It is all in the past now, *chérie*, Anne is free now, a widow and her own mistress."

"You think they will marry?"

"She does not tell me of her plans, Georgianna, but . . ." He shrugged significantly and Georgianna understood. There was no need for words. Merely to see them together was enough. She knew she should have felt happy for both their sakes that now they could be together, but instead there was a crushing weight of despair against her heart. "Georgianna?" Philippe's voice was a husky whisper

155

against her ear. There was a look, both pleading and determined, in his eyes. She knew he was going to kiss her. It was in the air; the very breeze that stirred the trees seemed to whisper it to her. She quivered a little and then went still as his arms enfolded her, and the ready laughter sprang to his eyes.

"It is nothing, *chérie*. You need not fear, I promise you." His lips were only inches from her own now, quirking in his ready smile. "Indeed people have been known to enjoy it."

She trembled, closing her eyes as she felt him gather her up against him, and then his lips were on hers, light and tender, with none of the bruising ferocity of that other kiss.

"See, it is not so very dreadful after all."

The understanding in his eyes was more than she could bear. He knew; somehow, he knew.

"Oh Philippe."

He ignored the delicate color sweeping over her face, and continued as though she had said nothing. "You are very young, *petite*, and have yet to learn that there are kisses and kisses." He paused meaningfully. "I hope that this one might wipe from your memory another, less pleasant." In the same even tone he continued, "Believe me, if it were in my power, I should make the gentleman concerned pay very dearly."

The soft tones became unusually clipped, as Georgianna started a little, her heart thumping uncomfortably.

"I am right aren't I, *petite*? It was Saint-Vire?"

Her expression gave her away.

"*Dieu!*" He leaned toward her, adding another word under his breath, his expression suddenly grim.

Georgianna shivered, frightened by what she read in his eyes.

"You shiver. You are frightened? Poor child. You have no need to be frightened of me, Georgianna. No need at all." Gently he reassured her, talking softly, allowing her to recover her composure. He was so kind, so understanding. His kiss all that the other had not been. Why then should she still remember the touch of hard lips against her own?

"Oh Philippe."

She swayed toward him, more in gratitude and relief than anything else, and was glad to rest against his shoulder. His voice was a soothing murmur against her ear as he waited for her trembling to cease. She felt his lips again against her brow in the lightest of caresses, and then the peace of the afternoon was shattered.

"Georgianna!"

She shrank within the circle of Philippe's protecting arm, turning agonized eyes in the direction of her guardian.

"So this is how you entertain yourselves, is it? Very pretty."

Slowly Philippe removed his arm, a new hard note Georgianna had never heard before in his voice, his eyes no longer laughing.

"*Petite*, return to Madame. Your guardian and I have much to discuss." Wordlessly she obeyed them, shivering anew as she intercepted the glances they exchanged.

157

"So, du Plessis, I trust I arrived in time?"

Philippe ignored the jibe.

"Or was it that you thought I was likely to be otherwise engaged? It was a shrewd move to include Anne in your party, but then I forgot that I am dealing with an expert." His lip curled over the last word.

Philippe still had not moved. His own voice was as emotionless as Saint-Vire's was charged. "Before you start, Saint-Vire, let me warn you, it was not what you thought."

The Marquis sneered openly. "No? I should have thought the circumstances were plain enough. She was in your arms."

"Indeed; but then appearances can so often be deceptive, my friend." Their glances locked in combat.

"Meaning?" drawled the Marquis. He had himself under control now, the tension gone from his face, only his eyes betraying him.

"Meaning that you have not always treated her as a guardian should, my friend. You can hardly blame me for succumbing to temptation when you have already done so yourself."

Slowly Saint-Vire clenched and unclenched his fingers, but Philippe du Plessis continued to hold his gaze.

"She told you?"

Philippe shrugged. Now it was his turn to be scornful. "Hardly. She didn't need to. I knew by the fear in her eyes. Every time I touched her it showed, but now at least I believe she knows a kiss need not be a punishment. Poor child. Life has not been kind to her." There was no laughter in the blue eyes now. None at all. "*Dieu*, Saint-Vire, I could kill you for what you have tried to do to that child." His voice was grim. "What manner of man are you that you need to show her your hatred in such a way?"

The Marquis flinched, but made no attempt to defend himself. He was seeing himself through Philippe de Plessis' eyes, and it was not pleasant. Suddenly, with painful clarity, he remembered how the slight body had trembled in his arms; the accusations she had flung at him. What had she said? Her father had been content to ignore her.

Philippe du Plessis watched him in silence. "You see, my friend? Now when it is too late you realize." Philippe's eyes raked him scornfully. "You are a man to be pitied, Saint-Vire. I know not what devil drives you, but this time it has taken you too far. Believe me, were it not for the scandal, nothing would bring me greater pleasure than to meet you." He made a stiff bow.

"I leave Paris within the week to put my estates in order. When I return it will be my privilege to call upon you and formally offer for your ward's hand." He observed the look on Saint-Vire's face without a trace of pity, save only to murmur, "You see, my friend? Didn't I tell you it was already too late?" Wearily, as though he could not bear the burden of his own thoughts, the Marquis followed him from the glade.

Saint-Vire was silent throughout the return journey. Georgianna, who had told the Comtesse nothing of what had transpired in the small glade, and was still in fact unaware of Philippe's formal offer, shrank under what she thought was her guardian's anger. She was unwilling to meet his eyes and see the disgust that must surely be written there. His coldness was more painful than his bruising kiss had been, crushing her pride, until she longed to protest and tell him that it wasn't the way he imagined.

She wanted to make him see that . . . that what? She was too confused to know except that it had something to do with the gentle look on his face whenever he chanced to look at Anne and the pain that self-same look caused her. They were rolling through the *faubourgs* when the check string was pulled with an urgency that nearly unseated Georgianna. The carriage lurched to a standstill.

They had stopped outside one of the smaller houses. The Marquis opened the door and alighted, sauntering across the road.

It was left to Philippe to explain, curtly and briefly. "That is where Louise de Liveaurac lives." Georgianna could not quite conceal her surprise. What a strange afternoon it had been. First the Marquis, so tender with Anne, and then Philippe; she had never seen him in such a grim mood. He had become almost as formidable as Saint-Vire himself, and now this! Surely Philippe had said the liaison was over?

Philippe's thoughts were traveling along much the same lines, although for different reasons and with different conclusions. He fancied he knew well enough what had driven Saint-Vire to seek out the lady, and in the same circumstances might not he himself have sought oblivion in much the same manner?

Georgianna glanced across rather curiously at Anne. Of all of them, she seemed the least affected. Didn't she mind the Marquis leaving her to go to his mistress? Anne returned her glance with a serene smile that was particularly her own. Georgianna sighed. Perhaps when you were so much in love, and so sure of your love being returned, there was no room for mere petty jealousy. The thought was unaccountably painful.

Louise de Livaurac sank wearily into a chair; her mouth was petulant. "You are a fool, Jules. How could you be so stupid to think that you could be rid of Saint-Vire so easily? Only think of the danger. If you were to be discovered, it would be the rack!" She shuddered. From the moment they had been accosted by Saint-Vire on the road from Paris, she had pestered Jules until she had finally dragged the truth from her.

Now he frowned angrily at her. "It was the merest mischance. I would have succeeded if that wretched girl had not chanced to come along!"

Louise shivered at his tone. "*Dieu*, Jules. If the servants should hear, it could mean the Bastille for us both. Do you think Saint-Vire suspects?"

Jules Clary laughed harshly. His sister was ever a fool. "Suspects! Of course he does.

Why else would he stop us on the road and command that we return to Paris?"

"You are frightened of him," she accused.

"No, I am not frightened. It is merely that it is not wise to be away from court for too long. The King has a short memory for some things, and our faces may well become forgotten." He shrugged comprehensively. "We have too much to lose. Besides, Saint-Vire can prove nothing, whatever he might choose to suspect." His eyes narrowed craftily. "Next time we must be more certain."

Next time! Appalled, Louise stared at him. "Jules, you cannot!"

A flunkey interrupted their conversation. "There is a gentleman outside asking for you."

"A gentleman? What is his name?"

"His name, my dear Louise, is Saint-Vire."

She spun around, her face the color of the white-lead powder the ladies used to paint their complexions. There was a split second before anyone spoke.

The Marquis allowed the door to swing to gently, a savage smile glinting across his face. There was that aura about him of barely controlled fury.

"Who let you in?"

"Who else, my dear, but your so efficient servant? Am I to take it that my presence is unwelcome?" His anger had given way to a mood no less dangerous.

Louise de Liveaurac shivered again. He reminded her of a panther dark, sleek, and dangerous, circling his prey, and waiting for them to run.

Monsieur Clary leaped angrily to his feet and found himself being considered extremely disdainfully through a raised eyeglass.

"Unwelcome! You can doubt it? After the insult you gave my sister. An insult that I assure you I have not forgotten."

"Then it seems we are both blessed with good memories, doesn't it, Clary?" replied Saint-Vire.

There was an ominous pause.

"Why have you come here?"

The Marquis expelled his breath on a long sigh. "Why?" he asked gently. "Merely benevolent good nature and a concern for my fellow men."

Clary licked his lips. "Since when have you cared about me?"

"Oh, but I assure you, my dear Jules, that I do. Indeed I have thought of very little else for the past few days. In fact, it occurs to me that your position at court—I believe it is Groom of the Bedchamber—has become a little arduous for you."

"Arduous?" repeated Clary weakly.

"Indeed," reiterated the Marquis. "I believe for the sake of your health it might be as well if you were to resign it, and leave for a more healthy clime. In fact, I do believe I could go farther and say it is almost a necessity. For the sake of your health, you understand?"

Monsieur Clary understood all too well both the remark and the watchful predatory look that accompanied it. "And if I do not?" he inquired bravely.

"Why, then I fear I really must take steps to see that you are, shall we say, displaced."

Clary took refuge in bluster. "You are trying to threaten me!"

"My dear Jules, I beg you to reflect. Would I be so maladroit? I leave such things to others. No, this is just the merest of friendly warnings."

Louise de Liveaurac, who had listened to this interchange without a word, got to her feet and reached imploringly for the Marquis' arm. "Justin, I beg of you. It was all the veriest mistake."

The Marquis shook her off as he might have done a fly. He inclined his head slightly, the light reflecting the glitter of his eyes. "As you say, my dear, the veriest mistake. But an unfortunate one for you. I trust I make myself clear."

On this threatening note, the Marquis took his leave.

Louise turned on her brother furiously. "You fool. A fine mess we are in now."

"Threats, nothing more," muttered Clary. "You allow yourself to be overwhelmed by the man, my dear."

"I see, and you, on the contrary, are completely unafraid of him? You will have to do as he says and leave Paris."

He laughed shortly. "I think you mean 'we,' my dear. For if I leave Paris, you will come with me!"

"Me! But I had nothing to do with it," she stormed at him.

"No? Who will believe that? Saint-Vire certainly will not." She paced the room angrily, while her brother watched grimly. "You'll see. You will feel differently now that you are threatened. However, all is not lost yet. I shall think of something."

Chapter
8

The days flew by on winged heels. Philippe
was busily engaged on preparations for a visit
to his estates, and was continuing to treat
Georgianna with tender affection. Having told
her of his proposed visit and seen that she did
not understand the reason behind it, he pressed
the matter no farther. Etiquette forbade it.

For several days after the ill-fated picnic,
Georgianna had gone in dread of a summons
to see her guardian, but one never came. In
fact, she rarely saw him, but when she did he
seemed more remote and unapproachable than
ever. The Comtesse watched her grow pale
and unhappy, but the Comtesse was too wise to
ask questions. If the child wanted to confide in
her, she would.

Georgianna and Anne had grown very
close. The older girl was in the process of opening up her hotel—a time-consuming operation,
but when she had time to spare she would visit
Georgianna and the two would then spend
an hour or more in the Rose Salon. The Comtesse, wise in the ways of young ladies, left

them alone, and thus it was that Georgianna became the repository for certain confidences.

It seemed that Anne had not been happy in her marriage. "It was an arranged match you understand," she explained to Georgianna.

"My parents chose my husband when I was still in the cradle. We were married when I was sixteen, and he was fifty."

Georgianna bent over her stitchery, unwilling to betray her pity.

"Poor Georges, he was in ill health even then. We had to retire to his estates, but it was too late. Although he lived for many years, he was never more than an invalid. Not that he wasn't kind to me," she hastened to assure Georgianna.

It was Anne's turn to bow her head now. "Philippe may have told you already. Although I regretted Georges' ill health, for me it was never a true marriage. There was a matter of another attachment, but duty and . . ."

"I do understand," intervened Georgianna. "But now you are free." Delicately she left it at that. If Anne wished to confide her love for Saint-Vire, then doubtless she would do so.

"Yes, although I did not know until recently that he, too, still returns my regard and is free to . . ." She blushed anew.

Georgianna sighed. Who, knowing Anne, could not love her? She was perhaps not strictly beautiful, although she had a pleasing countenance, but her true beauty lay in her nature. No wonder Saint-Vire smiled for her as he never did for herself. Was this the reason the Marquis had always seemed so withdrawn? Unrequited love?

She looked at Anne's lips, parted in a dreaming smile. Had they ever been bruised by his anger? No, of course not. They would only have known his tenderness and respect. She stabbed the needle into the silk. She must not think in this fashion. It was pointless. But it was no use. The memory of that kiss was always with her; much more so now that she had experienced Philippe's tender embrace, and known the other for what it was. The dark, hawklike face had even begun to invade her dreams!

She had taken refuge from her thoughts in Philippe's company, but soon he would be leaving for the country, and even that would be denied her. How long before the Marquis announced his forthcoming marriage to Anne? Surely there could be no reason for them to delay? And it was plain to all the world how much he thought of her from the way he looked at her.

Georgianna sighed.

Anne's soft voice broke the silence. "So Philippe is taking you to the Grande Balle at Versailles. It should be quite an occasion. I remember when I was first at court. . . ." Her eyes grew dreamy, and Georgianna hesitated to intrude upon her private happiness.

"You are going?"

Anne shook her head, the soft brown ringlets dancing. "No."

She smiled secretly, and fresh pain lacerated Georgianna's heart.

Saint-Vire wasn't going either!

Other people had not been wasting time, as became evident when Jules Clary sauntered into his sister's salon. It seemed that Monsieur Clary was feeling well pleased with life, and it showed. Louise de Liveaurac, however, was far from happy. Since their return to Paris, there had been the most unwelcome call by Saint-Vire, one attendance at Versailles, where it had been more than clear that brother and sister were somewhat *persona non grata*—in some quarters at least and since then she had not set foot out of doors. Her dissatisfaction with life showed quite plainly in the petulant droop of her lips, jovially ignored by her brother.

"Ah, Louise, I find you well, I trust?"

Since this was so obviously not the case, Louise treated him to a display of sulky temper. "Well enough I suppose, to say you are my first visitor in days. We might as well have stayed in the country. Life is so dull. No one to talk to! I daren't set foot outside lest I am ignored by an acquaintance." One small foot tapped angrily on the floor. "It is all Saint-Vire's doing, of course. *Tiens*, but I could almost wish your hired assassin had done away with him!"

Her brother smiled in evident enjoyment. "I am pleased to hear you say so, Louise, and as for the rest, soon, my dear, the boot could well be on the other foot. Indeed, if you play your cards well, even the highest in the land will be seeking your favor."

The impatient foot stilled. "What are you talking about, Jules?"

He stretched full length in the chair, every line of his body expressing satisfaction. "I am talking, my dear Louise, about a little plan I have evolved. One might almost call it a plan for killing two birds with one stone."

"And does this plan involve Saint-Vire?" inquired his sister waspishly.

"How very astute of you, my dear. It most assuredly does."

Louise sighed.

"I wish you would put Saint-Vire out of your mind."

She shivered slightly. "He frightens me, especially now. It would be foolish to try to kill him again. Even if you succeeded, if you were to be found out . . ."

"Ah, but you see, Louise, that is the charm of my plan. I shall not be found out, and this time, right shall be on our side. But, there, I digress, allow me to tell you the tale in my own way."

Seldom had Louise seen her brother in such a good mood. His high spirits were in direct contrast to her own feelings, and with unusual sarcasm she drawled,

"By all means, brother, it will while away the time, if nothing else."

"You may mock, Louise, but if I succeed, and I intend to, you could well become the foremost woman in all France." The words seemed to tremble on the air.

Louise paled, and then flushed, her bad temper completely forgotten. "And if it fails?"

"It won't," Jules assured her, pulling his chair closer to hers, lowering his voice a little. "At last I believe our luck is changing, and when it does, those who have scorned and mocked us will count the cost dearly."

Louise frowned. All this barely suppressed excitement and talk of luck was quite unlike her normally dour brother. So was his air of important secrecy. She did not know what to make of it. "I don't understand."

"You will. By the greatest of good fortune I happened to come across Maurepas the other night."

Louise sighed. Where was all this leading? "So you saw the King's First Minister. What of it? One may see him every day at Versailles, or hadn't you noticed?"

Jules ignored the jibe. "We had a most interesting conversation."

Louise yawned affectedly, determined to be provoking. It was entirely Jules' fault that she was cooped up here. If he hadn't been foolish enough to cross Saint-Vire, there would be no necessity for all this fuss. Conveniently she forgot her own part in the Saint-Vire affair. However, it seemed that nothing could annoy Jules.

"You know how Maurepas hates La Pompadour?"

"Of course. The whole of France knows, but it avails him little. He might be the King's First Minister, but it is La Pompadour who wields the real power."

Jules smiled thinly.

"At the moment, yes, but Maurepas had been drinking and was in the mood for confidences."

"And what pray, dear brother, did he confide in you?"

He was too intent on his tale to notice the sarcasm. "He told me, Louise, that he considered it time Louis had another, and shall we say, a more accommodating mistress!"

Louise's lip curled. "*Dieu*, Jules, that has been tried before many times. For one night, or even two perhaps, it might work, but he always returns to La Pompadour."

"As you say, it has been tried before with pretty sluts. This time it would be different, this time it would not be a little *fille de joie*, but a woman of wit and intelligence, well born and beautiful. In short, my dear, yourself."

The fingers that idly smoothed the satin of her gown shook a little. To be the King's mistress, and not merely his mistress, but the new *maitress en titre*. The prospect was dazzling. Her fingers clenched on the satin, uncaring that she was crushing it. How those who had so rashly followed Saint-Vire's lead and ignored her would regret their actions. She smiled slowly, while Jules watched, well pleased. He had judged his sister's reaction to a nicety, he thought.

"And Saint-Vire, where does he fit into all this?"

Jules laughed mirthlessly. "Ah yes, I was wondering when you would ask that. I am relieved, my dear, to discover that you have recovered your normal good sense. In return for assisting Maurepas to displace La Pompadour, he is prepared to be very generous."

"So?"

"So, my dear, his generosity will take the form of granting us a *lettre de cachet,* or to be more precise, two. . . ."

She went white and then started to tremble from head to foot as his words sank in. No one in France, be they high or low, could hear the dreaded words *lettre de cachet* without flinching in fear. Issued by the King's First Minister, and signed by the King himself, it was the most dangerous privilege of French royalty, for it condemned the recipient to imprisonment in the Bastille forever. It was never revoked, and since the King never saw the name inscribed upon it there was no appeal. It had been the means of crushing many a noble family, or an out-spoken politician, and even a recalcitrant peasant. The *lettre de cachet* was no respecter of class or creed; it embraced all men with the icy caress of death. No wonder Louise de Liveaurac shuddered.

"*Dieu,* Jules, you would do that?"

"I would do anything, and everything, to be revenged upon Saint-Vire, especially in such a delightful manner."

Louise shivered. "But you said two?"

"Ah yes, a rather pleasing refinement, I thought. It is rumored that Saint-Vire is passing fond of that ward of his. While he is in the Bastille he will have plenty of time on his hands. Thinking of the girl sharing his fate, perhaps even only separated from him by a stone wall, will doubtless help to pass some of it."

"He will go mad!"

"*Vraiment!* I hope he may do so."

Louise paced the room, her bottom lip caught between her teeth. She had no love for Saint-Vire now, but she shrank from inflicting such an appalling fate on him. However, she could not afford to be sentimental—there were plenty of other women who would leap at the chance of becoming the King's mistress. In any case, if she refused to assist she knew just how unpleasant her brother could be. . . .

Jules watched her gloatingly. She would not refuse. The temptation would be too great. Besides, he would not allow her to. How grand life would be as the brother of Louis' mistress. He savored the thought like a drunkard might a bottle of wine.

"What do I have to do?" Louise asked slowly.

Jules smiled. "Nothing. Maurepas has it all in hand. Louis' normal valet will be taken ill with a stomach upset," he told her. "Maurepas will provide a substitute. From then on, it is quite simple. When Louis retires after the *coucher*, you will be waiting for him. The valet will let you in." Jules shrugged expressively. "After that, my dear sister, it will be up to you and I trust you will not let us down."

Louise did not bother to reply. What an opportunity. Mistress of the King!

"When?"

"The sooner the better."

"And Saint-Vire?" she asked uneasily.

"There is to be a *grande balle* in the grotto at Versaille tomorrow, costumed in the Greek fashion to fit the mood of the grotto. We shall be there, and so will Maurepas. It will be quite easy for him to pass the *lettres* to us."

Louise shivered. "I don't like it, Jules. Let Saint-Vire be, or at least wait until I am Louis' mistress.

"No. It will be done my way, sister, but it need not concern you. You concentrate on the King." He paused for a second at the door. "Until tomorrow then, Louise."

Louise pulled the bell rope and waited for her maid to appear.

"Ah, Jeanette. There is to be a ball at Versailles tomorrow, I shall be attending. I shall need a suitable costume. A water sprite or nymph, you understand."

These orders given, Louise sat back in her chair. She had not forgotton the tale of how Madame de Pompadour had appeared in the Galerie des Glaces at a masked ball and captured the attention and the heart of the King of France. That had been nearly twenty years ago, though, and it was time he lost his heart elsewhere.

Georgianna hurried downstairs. She was already late and the Comtesse had had to order dinner to be set back an hour. Still she was ready now; just her cloak to put on. Philippe had warned her that it could be cold in the grotto. Since the afternoon of the picnic she had begged Philippe not to come to the hotel, and while he had been none too pleased, he had acceded to her wishes. She had little wish to precipitate a quarrel between her guardian and Philippe. As she reached the bottom of the stairs a figure detached itself from the shadows.

"Saint-Vire!"

She stumbled, and would have fallen had it not been for the steel fingers enclosing her wrist. It struck her that he was like a hawk, dark-visaged and secret, waiting to pounce on the unwary.

"Georgianna."

He purred her name, the word soft with hidden menace, sending a *frisson* of fear down her spine. Why must he be like this with her?

"So, you go to Versailles with du Plessis? You will be able to restrain your emotions enough to ensure that there is no repetition of the so-tender scene I surprised the other day, I trust?"

Her hands curled into her palms. How could he be so hateful? With a few drawled words he had turned what had been a moment of shared sweetness and wonder into something sordid and hidden.

His eyes mocked her.

"Well, have you nothing to say?"

"Nothing to you!" She wished her voice did not have that betraying tremble. What would he be doing while they were at Versailles? She dared not risk the question lest it called forth again his lashing sarcasm.

The King had arranged for his guests to be ferried to the grotto, where the ball was to be held, by water. They were to travel along the Grand Canal using the Venetian Galleys that formed part of his miniature fleet.

Waiting to board one of the vessels, Georgianna reflected ruefully that she must indeed be growing satiated with pleasure, for despite the delights promised by the evening she was finding it hard to raise much enthusiasm. Again and again her thoughts would return to her guardian, producing that now familiar little ache in the region of her heart. She wished fervently that he might bestow upon her just one of the smiles he gave so freely to Anne.

At her side the Comtesse frowned. "Are you all right, child?"

She was rewarded with a rather wan smile. "Just a megrim, nothing more, it will soon be gone."

At last they were able to take their seats in the galley, and even Georgianna's low spirits were not proof against the scene that met their eyes as they traversed the canal.

The banks were illuminated by tiers of glittering lights, arranged in such a manner as to form blue-and-gold *fleurs de lis,* the heraldic emblem of the monarch of France. Later the Comtesse whispered that there would be fireworks, a truly magnificent sight!

Georgianna was too busy staring around wide-eyed to take in her words. Surely there could be nothing in the world to compare with Versailles.

"Wait until you see the grotto," she was advised by the Comtesse.

And rightly so. It defied description. As

they stepped from the galley she could hear the sound of water mingling with the music. Below them the entire grove glowed with a thousand lanterns, sparkling from the trees like colored glowworms.

"Oh, it's lovely!"

"I quite agree." It was Philippe, laughing down at her, making her blush rosily as she realized it was her face he was looking at and not the grove.

Like herself he was wearing evening dress, but she soon realized they were among the minority. Most of the guests sported floating draperies of Grecian design, and Georgianna couldn't help blushing a little as she realized that some of the costumes were far from modest!

All around the edge of the grove were striped silk tents and pavilions. "For those among the guests who prefer a little privacy," Philippe whispered. "And now if Madame will entrust you to me, perhaps some wine and then a dance?"

The Comtesse signified her agreement. Let Justin say what he wished, Philippe was definitely in love with the child.

"Well, *petite*, you seem a little somber. Dare I hope my imminent departure has anything to do with that sad smile?"

Georgianna was able to reply quite honestly that it had. Only she knew that that was not the whole truth.

"If it consoles you, *chérie*, you cannot miss me more than I shall miss you." He raised her fingers to his lips, holding them for a while and looking deep into her eyes. He was prevented from saying anything further to Georgianna by the arrival of the Prince du Conde.

The Prince looked from Philippe to Georgianna. "My presence is obviously not very welcome."

"No," came the brief response.

"My apologies, my friend, but La Pompadour is asking after you."

Philippe sighed. "If you will excuse me for a moment, Georgianna. Wait here, I shall return as soon as I can."

"I shall keep her company, du Plessis," offered the irrepressible Conde.

"Oh no. You, *mon ami*, will accompany me," declared Philippe firmly. "Come."

Their bantering brought a smile to Georgianna's lips. Philippe was a dear, and she was becoming increasingly fond of him.

Left to her own devices, she wandered in the direction of the tents. A particularly ornate one in lavender and white caught her eye, possibly because it was one of the largest. It wasn't until she was right outside it that she realized it was occupied. Embarrassed, she was just starting to edge away when someone spoke.

"Well, do you have them?"

It was a man's voice, elusively familiar, and charged with impatience. Where had she heard it before? Georgianna paused, frowning.

A second man spoke. "Yes, they are both here."

She heard the crackle of parchment and again that familiar voice, "Oh excellent, Maurepas, excellent!"

"And you have arranged the other matter?" There was a moment's silence and then, "Indeed, my sister is honored to be chosen, aren't you, my dear?"

"Yes," came the answer.

It was only one word, but it was sufficient. Georgianna recognized her voice instantly, and abandoned any pretense of not listening. The woman inside the tent was Saint-Vire's ex-mistress, the woman he had insulted at Versailles.

Suddenly she knew where she had heard the man's voice before. It was her brother. The man who had challenged her guardian. A shiver ran down her spine.

"Excellent," spoke the second man again.

He had lowered his voice, so that she had to strain to hear what he was saying.

"Well, it is for tonight then. Everything has worked out very well. I predict even at this moment La Pompadour and the valet are both beginning to feel a little unwell!"

"You are sure everything will go according to plan?" asked Louise.

"Quite sure," came the reassuring response. "Now I think it is best that I leave. It wouldn't do for people to know of our association—not yet at least. I wish you luck, my dear." Monsieur Clary spoke again, his voice harsh with suppressed emotion. "Are the *lettres* in order?"

The reply came mockingly, "But of course, my dear Jules. Two *lettres de cachet* are what I think we agreed upon. They are both there, as you have seen. You see how high I rate your services, Clary. Many people would pay thousands of *livres* for just one. The Comte de Saint-Vire will doubtless be surprised to receive his."

Georgianna started. Why were they mentioning her guardian? She caught the hiss of indrawn breath.

"Saint-Viere? What makes you think it is he?"

Again came that mocking laugh. "My dear Clary, nothing is secret from me, and you would do well to remember that. It will make our association so much pleasanter."

He was leaving. Hurriedly Georgianna started to move away. She must not be found here eavesdropping.

She caught sight of Philippe's golden head and hurried toward him, her mind in turmoil. What were these *lettres?* And how did they affect her guardian? Alarm bells rang deep within her, triggered off by the unmistakable gloating she had heard in Monsieur Clary's voice. How he must hate the Marquis. Desperately she tugged at Philippe's sleeve, her eyes darkening with anxiety.

"Oh Philippe!"

His hand steadied her reassuringly.

"*Chérie?* Something is wrong?"

She bit her lip, striving to appear calm.

"Philippe, what is a *lettre de cachet?*"

Even in the dim half light she could see the shock ripple through him, shock he tried hard to hide; she could feel it in the sudden tensing of the fingers beneath her elbow.

"A *lettre de cachet?*" he reiterated carefully, repeating her words as though even to utter them caused him actual physical pain.

Georgianna glanced upward. The normally laughing eyes were dark and somber, no vestige of humor in the handsome face. She shivered and whispered, "Philippe, what is wrong?" Even to her own ears, her voice sounded strained. "Tell me quickly," she implored, her own fears increasing tenfold as she realized with sickening dread that Philippe—laughing, irrepressible Philippe—was frightened. It was there, lurking in the darkness of his eyes, in the clenched muscles of his arm, and in the wry twist of his lips.

She allowed him to lead her gently into the welcoming shadows of a tree. Here they could talk unseen. When at last he turned to face her it was obvious that he was in the grip of some strong emotion.

"Where did you hear those words, Georgianna?"

She had to lean forward to catch the question, and then when she would have replied he held up a hand to forestall her.

"No. God forgive me, but I really would rather not know."

He saw her expression and smiled bitterly.

"A coward, am I not?"

She did not bother to answer. Only one thing concerned her now, and that was her guardian.

"Philippe, please!"

Never had she known such fear. All very well for Philippe to call himself a coward—she knew that was something he was far from being, and that knowledge only increased her own dread.

"Very well, *petite*. Since you ask, I shall tell you. But I could wish you had chosen a more pleasant topic of conversation." His mouth twisted again. "The *lettre de cachet* lies over the land of France like an open sore. It is an abomination. . . ." He half turned from her, sighing. "And yet for all that, there is not one man in the entire Kingdom who would dare speak against it."

"But what is it?"

The agonized whisper brought him back to face her. His hands reached out and held her arms. "I shall not ask who your concern is for. I believe I can guess." Bitterness edged his voice, and although she flushed a little, Georgianna made no attempt to contradict him. "Very well then, but you must be brave, Georgianna."

She moistened her lips, her heart thudding heavily.

"The *lettre de cachet* means a living death; it is imprisonment in the Bastille."

His words hung on the air, menacing and unrecallable. Even Georgianna had heard of that dreadful prison into which people disappeared, never to be seen again. She just could not take it in. She shook her head, trying to clear her muddled thoughts.

"But why? How?"

Philippe shrugged. "It is quite simple. The *lettre* signed by the King is an authority to imprison whoever the holder of the *lettre* wishes. None can escape it, and it is never rescinded." The quietly spoken words fell into the silence.

Georgianna struggled to understand the

enormity of Philippe's words. "But surely the King would not harm an innocent person?" She was unaware of the hysterical note in her voice, but as Philippe's grasp of her arms tightened, she could feel him trembling, and knew it was all too true.

"My dear, I'm very sorry." Carefully he avoided her eyes. He hesitated and then continued roughly, "*Dieu*, that you should be mixed up in all this. Would to God that there was something I could do, but . . ." He shrugged despairingly.

Even though Philippe's shock and dread were better concealed than her own, they were still there. Surely she must be in the grip of some dreadful nightmare, and yet deep within her she acknowledged the truth of his words, as though it was something she had sensed all along.

This was no nightmare. . . . It was all too frighteningly true!

Louise and her brother had somehow obtained a *lettre de cachet* to incarcerate her guardian in the Bastille!

Her heart gave a frightened bound. "Philippe, how is this *lettre* enforced?" In the darkness she caught the soft gleam of Philippe's eyes, felt the warmth of his hands as they enclosed hers. His voice was grim.

"By Louis' guard, without warning. There is no chance of escape."

Her heart hammered against her ribs, so painfully she could barely breathe. Fear made her mouth dry. Her guardian was in danger. Grave danger. She must tell him! She did not stop to question her instinctive desire to save him. She only knew she must return to the hotel Saint-Vire at once.

"Philippe, I must warn him."

No need to ask who. Philippe gave her a look, half sorrowful, half bitter, but wholly understanding. "If that is the way of it, *petite*, although I could wish it were otherwise."

With her mind on her guardian, she scarcely heard his words. She must find the Comtesse. They must leave. Oh God, please let them be in time. Her whole body was trembling like an aspen, her eyes wide with fear. Philippe knew better than to question her. When a *lettre de cachet* was involved, it was better not to know too much.

He touched her gently on the arm. "My carriage is at your disposal, Georgiana. It would be best, I think, not to worry Madame."

Chapter
9

Outside the hotel all was peaceful. Did that mean there was still time? Or—Georgianna could not prevent the thought—were they already too late?

Philippe helped Georgianna from the carriage. Then there was just the faint touch of his lips against her hair before she slipped from his arms, unaware that their embrace had been observed.

Jacques was in the hall.

"Is my guardian in?" she asked. Her heart pounded as she waited for the reply.

"Yes, I believe he returned not half an hour ago, miss. He is in his room."

Ignoring the man's startled looks, Georgianna ran up the stairs, not stopping until she was outside his door. Oblivious to the conventions, and with only the sketchiest of knocks, she burst into his room. His valet stared disapprovingly at her.

"What is it, Pierre?" She heard Saint-Vire's voice from the dressing room.

"It is I, Georgianna."

"What!"

He came into the room, looking none too pleased, and hot on the heels of her initial relief came paralyzing embarrassment as she realized he had been in the act of disrobing. He was standing in his stocking feet, his shirt carelessly unfastened.

"I have to see you. It is important." Even to her own ears her voice sounded strangely weak. "Please!"

One raised eyebrow dismissed the hovering valet, and she heard the faint click of the door as he left.

"So, you wanted to see me? What was it that couldn't wait until morning? Has the besotted Philippe proposed?

"Oh, please, we haven't much time." Her voice was an agonized whisper.

The dancing light from the tapers threw shadows across the warm brown of his chest, the light mesmerizing her. He was at her side, his arms hanging loosely. "It is not Philippe then?"

She shook her head, unable to speak.

Some of the tension seemed to leave his body. He half turned from her so that his face was in the shadows. "You surprise me." He swung back staring down into her frightened eyes with brooding intensity. "So then, what can it be, I wonder, that prompts you to beard the lion in his den?" His mouth twisted bitterly. "Aren't you afraid I might forget myself and repeat the insult I have already given you, especially since you come to me straight from Philippe's kisses?" He lingered unpleasantly over the words, while her mind screamed in agony. How could she tell him when he persisted in talking like this? Angrily she cut across his words.

"Stop it! Stop it! This has nothing to do with Philippe or when you kissed me. You must listen to me." In her fear for him she caught at his arm, flushing as he pulled away from her.

"It's Monsieur Clary."

"Clary?"

She had his attention now. "Yes, I heard him at Versailles. He was talking about you, and about a *lettre de cachet*." She stumbled a little over the words. "I asked Philippe what they were and he told me."

"They?" The word was sharp.

"Yes, Monsieur Clary had two. Oh please, hurry, you must leave. They may arrive at any moment." There was no mistaking the agony in her voice.

Somberly he stared down at her, looking as though he was seeing her for the first time. "So, after all I have done to you, you still come to warn me. It didn't occur to you that perhaps the Bastille might be a fitting fate for me?"

"You are my guardian, I couldn't . . ." She shivered anew.

There was an expression in his eyes she could not read. "So Monsiur Clary would imprison me in the Bastille, would he? Well, we shall outwit him yet." He looked at her for a moment. "We must hurry then, we shall need to be on our way within the hour."

"We?" She stared uncertainly at him.

"Yes, both of us. Who did you think the other *lettre* was intended for?"

She moistened her lips nervously. "But why me?"

"You are my ward. Doubtless Clary thinks it amusing to incarcerate us both. Now quickly we have no time to lose. The sooner we reach England the better."

"But what about Anne?"

"Anne?" He glanced sharply at her.

"You can't leave her now. You were going to be married."

She stepped backward as he advanced slowly.

"Were we so?"

"You love her, and she loves you." Her heart was thumping wildly.

Why was he looking at her in that strange manner? "And who told you that?"

"Philippe. He told me how you first loved her when you came from England but that she was betrothed to another, and now that you are both free. . . ." Her voice died away.

"As a friend, nothing more, and I am most certainly not the man she is going to marry. That is someone else," he told her in a voice devoid of any emotion.

"But you seemed so close. You were so loving to her."

He looked at her and then away. "In time you will learn that there are many different sorts of love; the one I felt for Anne was not that of a man for the woman he wants to share his life with."

The words fell into a pool of silence, reverberating through Georgianna's mind. "Have you ever felt that love for anyone?" she asked.

It seemed he would never answer. He looked at her, his eyes veiled. "No!" The word was a harsh denial.

In the candlelight she caught the flutter of his shirt as though he was having difficulty controlling his breathing.

"Come, there is no time to waste on pointless discussion; we must be on our way."

"But Madame?"

"Claudine will be safe enough, never fear. I'll have the carriage brought around. Don't wake your maid. The fewer people concerned with this the better."

Georgianna barely had time to stuff a few things into her dressing case before he was back.

"I have given Jacques a note for Claudine. Are you ready?" She nodded, trying to appear calm. It didn't seem possible. Only an hour before she had been dancing and now they were creeping out of Paris like thieves in the night!

Paris was sleeping; nothing stirred in the streets. With every corner Georgianna half expected to see Louis' guard confronting them. She and Saint-Vire flew northward, barely checking as the carriage raced along the narrow streets, but this time with grim purpose; the thundering of the magnificent horses' hooves no louder or more insistent than her own pulse. As they swung out of Paris, never checking at the city gate, she realized she was gripping the edge of her seat so hard that her fingers were white to the very bone.

"Will we make it?"

The Marquis turned to look at her, his face shadowed. "It's too soon to say yet. Clary may wait until morning, but on the other hand, he may not, and we have still to reach the coast."

"And if they catch us?"

With a brief gesture he allowed his cloak to fall open, revealing the dull steely glint of dueling pistols in the inside pocket. His fingers curled around one.

"If all else fails, if we cannot lose them on the road, or bribe them, then I shall use these."

"You mean you will shoot them!"

Again she saw the brooding, intense look on his face.

"Not them—us."

It took her several seconds to gauge the full meaning of his words, and only then did she realize the true nature of their plight.

"Believe me, it would be infinitely preferable to the Bastille, but if you wish, you may choose to go with Clary. Who knows, you may be able to use other methods of persuasion?"

Georgianna could not repress a shudder of horror.

"I would rather die!"

"That's what I thought."

Strangely enough, for once the laconic drawl did not annoy her, and it struck her that if she must endure this nightmare situation, there was no one she would rather endure it with. She glanced at her guardian. Despite his dislike of her and her own fear of him, she knew in that moment that if anyone could save them it was he. Some of her fear left her. Whatever lay ahead, at least they would meet it together. The thought was comforting.

The miles flew by. They stopped to change horses. Once. Twice. They were over halfway there. The long, flat road stretched ahead of them. Dawn broke in a mist of gray, turning to rose pink and finally clear, fresh blue as the sun edged over the horizon. It was day!

Whenever Georgianna looked back, the road was empty. She prayed it might remain so until they reached Calais. In the face of her guardian's apparent calm she was reluctant to voice her own fears, and so the miles crept by.

They were well past Abbeville now, their last change. Every mile was an agony of suspense for Georgianna, her ears stretched for the first sounds of pursuit, every muscle strained to the breaking point, as though somehow to remain so lent them speed. Taut as a bowstring, again and again her eyes swept the empty road. How much longer?

At last they crested a slight incline and there below them lay Calais, a huddle of grimy buildings, the Channel a dirty gray-green, and yet so very welcome. The carriage checked and then began the descent, until they could see through the houses the ungainly pacquet, bobbing at anchor on the flooding tide.

"We're here!" Wonder and disbelief mingled in the words.

The Marquis smiled grimly. "Yes, and luck it seems is with us. The pacquet should be leaving on the tide."

Georgianna glanced doubtfully at it. "How do you know?"

"See how it sits heavily in the water? Well laden by the looks of it."

It seemed a truce had been declared between them. Either that, or his concern for their safety outweighed his animosity toward her. She had no means of knowing which.

The carriage swept down to the harbor, throwing up a cloud of dust. The horses were exhausted and well lathered.

"Wait here while I see the captain."

He wasn't gone long. It was only a matter of minutes, although it seemed like hours to Georgianna waiting in the carriage.

"Is it all right?"

He smiled thinly. "The captain is all obliging. They have found us a cabin. The meanest the boat possesses, I believe." He stared out to sea, his expression forbidding. "We shall have to share it."

Georgianna was too tired to see what caused the look. Was it the fact that it was not perhaps *comme il faut,* or a dislike of any possible intimacy between them?

Georgianna stood in the stern watching the land slowly disappear, the deck heaving slightly beneath her feet. Suddenly she saw them. Half a dozen riders on the skyline, the sun glinting brightly on the gold braid of their uniforms, picking out the emblazoned lillies of France.

She dragged her eyes away from the shore, unable to believe they were really safe. Relief, heady as a glass of wine, coursed through her veins. She must tell her guardian and share the moment of triumph with him.

He was in the small cramped cabin that was all he had been able to obtain despite the payment of goodly sum of money, but the Captain was no fool. There was only one reason why well-heeled noblemen desired to leave France in such a hurry that they came with neither baggage nor attendants, and that being the case, doubtless a few hours of discomfort was a small price to pay.

The cabin was airless, unpleasantly so after the cool sea breeze, but Georgianna barely noticed.

"Saint-Vire." Impulsively she rushed to his side, her face alight. "The King's men, they've just ridden into Calais. Thank goodness they came too late. You've saved us! If it hadn't been for you . . ."

"I have no use for your gratitude," he told her harshly. The rocking motion of the boat caught her off guard, throwing her against him. She thought she caught a muttered curse, and then arms went around her, a look of helpless bitterness in his eyes as he pulled her to him and his mouth came down on hers, blotting out coherent thought. His touch was a revelation. Where she should have experienced hatred and anger, she felt only joy. It surged through her veins like a triumphant flood, destroying the barriers she had raised in her mind. For a moment she fought against it and him, but both were too powerful. She thought she caught her name, murmured under his breath, a tremor in his body, something that was half sigh, half groan, before she was swept away. At last she admitted what she had been trying to deny for weeks. She did not hate him. How could she? She loved him! She trembled with the knowledge, and instantly she was free. In the dark of the cabin she flushed vividly. What must he think?

"I'm sorry!"

"You're sorry!" He stared at her in exasperation.

Her flush deepened. "We were both overwrought." She shrugged helplessly. "The journey . . . the worry. . . ."

There were hard lines either side of his mouth. "Go on. What other excuses can you make for me? You came down here to thank me for saving your life, wasn't that it? Shall I tell you just how worthy of your thanks I really am? Do you know the life I had planned for you as my ward?" His hands gripped her shoulders. "Well, I shall tell you. You were to be the instrument of my revenge upon my father. You were to expiate my guilt and appease my conscience." His eyes were hard, as though he wanted to shock her.

Georgianna listened to what he said without flinching and then quite calmly, as though it excused him of everything, told him: "Yes, I know all about it. Claudine told me about your mother."

In the faint light his face was shadowed, hidden. "*Dieu!* And still you saved my life?"

"It was not as you thought. I tried to tell you. My father," she turned away, "my father cared nothing for me." She could not continue.

His hands dropped from her shoulders. He sounded very tired. "Indeed you must pity me, Georgianna. Your forbearance has been that of a healthy child for its crippled companion." His voice was bitter. "I see how I have no need to ask your forgiveness for what I have just done. Doubtless you already know the reason for it." Slowly he walked past her.

She tried to rest and could not, reliving over and over again that moment in his arms. Whatever it had meant to her, she could not pretend that it had been anything other than a momentary impulse for him, and yet she would not have had it any different. At least it had been prompted, however fleetingly, by desire, rather than anger, and that knowledge alone was vaguely comforting. She liked Philippe and always would, but she knew now she could never love him. What was it her guardian had said? There here many different types of love. But there was only one that mattered.

Georgianna lay on the small bunk, her thoughts drifting with the rocking of the boat. She loved Saint-Vire! Where would it all lead? To unhappiness eventually for her, certainly. Behind them lay France and the past; ahead, London and the future. Was it perhaps too much to hope that his hatred of her, too, was now in the past? Georgianna sighed. She remembered the look on his face when she had told him that her father had not cared for her as he imagined. For a moment she had thought she saw anger, and something else—was it regret? She sighed again. She must be a victim of her own imagination. Her guardian had no regrets for what was past. Why should he have? At least some sort of truce seemed to have been declared between them, however fleeting, and she had his gratitude. Was that why he had kissed her? Out of gratitude? The thought was insupportable, and yet it had to be faced.

Suddenly, drowning in a maelstrom of new feelings, Georgianna longed to be once more the girl who had lived so quietly in the country. Where had that girl gone? The girl who had wanted only the love of a family.

The clatter of feet upon the companionway and the shout of "Land up ahead, miss" scattered her thoughts.

Soon they would be in England. Yes, she told herself silently, and shall I have to endure his mocking looks, his indifference, knowing all the while that I love him?

"Ah, Georgianna, there you are!"

Saint-Vire looked so normal and unconcerned. A painful lump settled in her throat.

People were streaming from the pacquet now. The air was full of cried greetings, the rattle of carriages, horses stamping their feet, curses and shouts from the sailors.

"Unless you are hungry I think we will avoid the inn. Doubtless our arrival will create a good deal of speculation in London anyway, without it being spoken abroad that we arrived without so much as a portmanteau between us."

The fact that she had no chaperone had barely intruded upon Georgianna's mind in her anxiety for their safety, but now she was forcibly and unpleasantly reminded of it. "I'm afraid I have been something of a nuisance."

His eyebrows shot up, his face distinctly forbidding. "Oh, no, my dear, I wouldn't say that. You have only disrupted my life completely, destroyed my carefully laid plans, turned my household into your champions and my aunt into my enemy, and forced me to leave a land I have lived in quite happily for a decade.'

The last accusation was unjust, and they both knew it. But the rest was untrue. If she had any pride, she told herself, she would refuse to go with him. She watched his tall figure stride away, and then on a sigh followed him.

The carriage was rolling toward London. In order to break the unnerving silence that had hung over them ever since they had left the coast, Georgianna asked, "When we arrive in London, what then?"

A dispassionate glance raked her. "I shall see you safely installed in Rossington House, take some lodgings, and then we shall sit back and wait."

"Wait?"

He sighed with the weary patience of one who is dealing with a small and not very bright child. "For Claudine to arrive, or had you forgotton? Unchaperoned you will not be accepted by London Society. They are just as strict in their own way as the French. Or perhaps I mistake the matter? Perhaps you do not care if the world calls you my mistress?"

Georgianna blanched. Not so much from shock, although his words had taken her by surprise, but from the disturbing picture his words painted. His mistress! She stole a glance at the strong profile, those firm lips that had possessed hers, those long fingers that had held her to him. She shivered with remembered delight, and instantly his eyes were mocking. "Besides, I'm sure Philippe, for one, would not be too pleased if our names were to be linked in such a manner."

"Philippe!" She had never given him a thought since they had left Paris. She flushed guiltily.

"So, I am right, you do care about him."

What should she say? Yes, she cared about him, but that it was nothing when compared to her love for him? She could picture the scorn in his eyes if she did.

Chapter
10

Night was drawing on when Georgianna and her guardian finally reached the outskirts of London. Link boys were already going about their duties, whistling cheerfully and calling raucously to one another. After the narrow streets of Paris, London seemed clean and spacious. The wind off the river was cool against Georgianna's skin as she peered from the windows. Even at this late hour the streets were thronged both with people and coaches. Across the river she caught the glitter of lights.

"Vauxhall Gardens," the Marquis told her laconically, where the *ton* flocked to amuse themselves.

They were rattling through one of the fine new squares now; a large house, illuminated by a hundred tapers, seemed to be the focus of many comings and goings. "Molly Carew's house. Doubtless she is holding another of her interminable rout parties," supplied the Marquis.

They had to wait quite fifteen minutes for the road to become free of carriages, and everywhere there were cries of: "My Lord Earl's carriage"; "My Lady's carriage"; "His Grace's coach."

Georgianna had never seen Rossington House before. As they entered the square for which it was named, she caught her breath in awe, and at her side the Marquis smiled sardonically.

"A fine sight, is it not?"

Georgianna could only nod dumbly. The house seemed to brood over the square, and unlike the one they had just passed, it seemed to repel rather than invite. The Marquis, with a very good idea of a stranger's first impression of his London home, drawled mockingly, "It was built by a gentlemen who served under Marlborough. For that he got the title, and being essentially a wise gentleman, he put it to good use."

"What did he do?"

"He found himself a rich wife and built this place."

Georgianna shivered. Perhaps it was the way he had told her, but it seemed such a cold, calculated thing.

It was obvious that her guardian had read her thoughts, for he continued, "Rather calculated, you think? But then you see he was not a gentleman who needed warmth of any sort in his life. As you will soon discover the place is like a tomb!"

As they swept into the hall, attended by sleepy and apologetic servants, Georgianna could see what he meant. All that marble, and the air! So cold, it practically bit into you.

Inside what was obviously the book room, it was a little better, especially when the servant put a light to the fire and closed the curtains. Their rich color gave an illusion of warmth, even if it was only that. As Georgianna glanced around she thought bleakly that this was not a happy house. She thought of the portrait in the Rose Salon in Paris. How that lovely girl must have hated it here!

A fresh thought struck her. She watched the Marquis drinking his wine.

"Were the first Marquis and his wife happy?"

"Together, do you mean? I doubt it. The Rossington's, as I'm sure my aunt has already told you, are not renowned for happy marriages, although his lasted for a shorter time than most. His heiress died after giving birth to his son."

Perhaps she had been lucky, she thought. She had escaped her unhappiness early, while his own mother . . . Somehow her thoughts must have betrayed her.

"You are thinking of my mother, no doubt. Claudine has obviously furnished you with most of the story, so perhaps you would like to hear the rest."

With mounting unhappiness she listened as he spoke of his parents.

"Your father did not love your mother then," she finally said timidly, almost fearing the dark tide of hatred she saw wash over him.

"Love! I sometimes used to think he hated her. It seemed my father loved the wife of one of his friends. Needing money, he married my mother. Barely a month after the wedding his friend died, leaving his wife a considerable heiress and free."

Georgianna's heart convulsed with pity. She made a slight move toward him and then checked. Now she understood it all. That small boy, watching his mother gradually fade away and not knowing why. The cold sternness of his father, locked away in his own private grief.

The Marquis' cold voice cut across these thoughts. "If you are preparing to indulge in a bout of sympathy for me, then do not. It is finished."

It might be finished, thought Georgianna, shivering, but the unhappiness lingered on in these rooms; she could almost feel it.

London, as Georgianna soon discovered, was crowded. It was the height of the season, all the nobility up from their country estates, filling their town houses with wives, children, and assorted relatives. The women were intent upon refurbishing their wardrobes and sampling everything London had to offer before returning to the wastes of Yorkshire, Cheshire, and wherever they had come from, and the men spent their days in the coffee houses and their nights at play in one of the innumerable gaming hells off Piccadilly.

However, the *ton* was not so occupied with its own affairs as to allow the arrival of the Marquis and his ward to pass unremarked. Before more than a couple of days were out, the news was flying around all the places where the *beau monde* gathered. It was being whispered in and out of the coffee houses, and between the acts of the latest play; sometimes in shocked accents, sometimes with a nod and a knowing wink. "Saint-Vire is back!"

"And with the prettiest chit seen in half a dozen years—says she is his ward, and that he intends to open up Rossington House." Every minute detail was avidly consumed as the rumors grew with each telling, until all the town knew that the Marquis had left Paris hurriedly, so hurriedly that the girl's chaperone had been left behind. (Here one or two gentlemen were rash enough to suggest that the omission might have owed more to design than to chance.)

The same question was on everyone's lips: "Why did they leave Paris in the first place?"

Since no one had as yet had the courage to ask the Marquis, they had to be content with mere speculation, and before too long it was being murmured behind raised fans that there had been talk in Paris about Saint-Vire's ward, so serious as to necessitate the fighting of a duel!

Dowagers glanced askance at one another. Wits wondered just how much or how little time the Marquis spent in those lodgings in Half Moon Street that he had so properly acquired for himself. Ladies enlivened their sedate carriage rides through the park by gossiping delightedly. However, although speculation on the true relationship between the Marquis and his ward, and the reason for their sudden arrival in their midst, was rife, no one knew the truth of the matter. All very well for one plump matron to whisper confidingly to another: "His ward? My dear—never! I knew him when he was a green lad. That year I spent in Paris, you remember? He was the most dreadful rake, I assure you."

All very well for Society to recall the Marquis' many and varied mistresses of the past; it was an unfortunate truth that in the matter of Miss Lawley, Saint-Vire was showing a new and very dull regard for the proprieties. Those gentleman who sworn that doubtless he returned to Rossington House when he thought the town asleep were soon disappointed to discover that his nights were spent chastely in his lodgings.

In fact, by the end of their first week in London, Georgianna had seen her guardian only twice. On both occasions it had been for little above half an hour, and even then it was in the company of the housekeeper. Yet each time she had been uncomfortably aware of the racing of her pulse and the rapid beating of her heart. Indeed, he had only to enter the room to send her spirits soaring dizzily, only to plummet again when he greeted her with his usual cool indifference. In many ways the time passed more slowly for Georgianna than for her guardian. He at least was free to come and go as he pleased, but he had impressed upon her that she was not so much as to set a foot out of doors until the Comtesse arrived, and so Georgianna found herself confined to the gloomy precincts of Rossington House and its garden, the dullness of her days enlivened only by her guardian's two brief visits.

Perhaps it was because she was so much alone that Georgianna's thoughts kept returning again and again to that kiss on the boat. She kept searching for a sign of tenderness that she might have overlooked, but finding none, sank into fresh despair. Even if his hatred of her had gone, there was no reason to suppose it would ever be replaced by love, and she knew now that nothing but his total love would ever be enough.

Perhaps it was just as well that the Friday after their arrival in London brought an end to her enforced confinement and, although Georgianna was unaware of it, a cessation to the gossip, squashing forever the outrageous tale that Georgianna far from being the Marquis' ward, was in fact his *chère amie*.

One very starchy dowager was heard to say to another that she had never believed it for one moment. Not even Saint-Vire would attempt such a very shocking course—trying to foist his mistress on polite society!

The incident that brought about these changes was the Comtesse's arrival in London at the latter end of a dull afternoon, when the pall of smoke hung over the city like a gray blanket.

Georgianna was in the library, poring over an extremely dull set of sermons, the only thing she could find to read in the vast room, and her attention had been wandering even before she heard the commotion in the hall.

With the eruption of another French lady several months before, and its unpleasant repercussions still fresh in his mind, the footman was not at first willing to allow the lady admittance, and it was the ensuing altercation that brought Georgianna to her feet. "Madame, you have come!"

Patently relieved, the footman stepped back, and the Comtesse swept into the room.

"*Tiens*, child. Thank goodness." The Comtesse wrinkled her nose. "What in the world is happening?" She gestured to the impassive footman. "Have the goodness to explain that I wish my bags to be taken up to my room immediately, and a hot bath prepared."

These orders given, the Comtesse embraced her warmly. "So you are well and happy? Saint-Vire has treated you well?"

Georgianna wasn't sure whether there was a slight hesitation before the last word. Her cheeks burned a little, and she avoided the question. "I am well, Madame; and you?"

"*Alors*, Georgianna. This English weather. Does it never stop raining in this accursed country?"

This was the Comtesse she remembered, but it seemed Madame had not finished her diatribe.

"Lud these Rossingtons. Their home is just like them. So austere, so cold." She shivered delicately. "'Tis just as well Justin takes after his Mama. You and he deal better together now, *chérie?*"

The astute eyes watched her, and Georgianna, who had been congratulating herself on her clever evasion of the earlier question, flushed again. "I don't see very much of him. He has taken lodgings." Frantically Georgianna gulped back the threatening sob.

"Oh, Madame!"

Warm arms opened to enfold her.

"There, child, don't cry."

At last when her tears had dried and she was more composed, the Comtesse asked gently, "So you love Saint-Vire, child?"

"Oh, Madame, what am I to do?"

The Comtesse smoothed back the tangled curls. "I take it Saint-Vire knows nothing of your feelings?"

Georgianna shuddered. "No, nor must he. I could not bear it."

For a moment the ladies were silent, and then on a slight sigh the Comtesse asked: "And what of Philippe? You know he is quite desolate, *chérie*? I have a letter for you from him. I shall give it to you later, but now I must rest." She paused on her way from the room. "By the way, if my nephew should arrive while I am sleeping, you may tell him I wish to see him."

Anxious fingers clutched at her arm. "You won't tell him?" pleaded Georgianna.

The Comtesse watched her sadly. "No, *cheri*, I won't. I promise you."

Georgianna drew a shuddering breath. She could not bear Saint-Vire to know she had committed the ultimate folly of falling in love with him, any more than she could bear the thought of his jeering rejection of that love. With the Comtesse at least, her secret was safe.

By the time the Marquis had arrived at White's, where he was engaged for the evening with a small party of friends, it was already all over the town that Saint-Vire's French aunt had arrived and was installed at Rossington House.

Sir Frederick Danvers, who was cutting the cards and dealing them with practiced ease, shot his friend an amused glance from beneath shaggy black eyebrows.

"Well, Justin? Are we to see this ward of yours now?" The Marquis picked up his cards, a faintly mocking smile touching his eyes. "And what exactly am I to understand from that remark, Freddy? I confess the significance of the word 'now' escapes me."

From the lanquid drawl it was difficult to know whether he was amused or merely bored, but Sir Frederick, who knew him as well as it was possible for any man to do, knew differently. He could recognize that faint edge of anger when he heard it.

"Come now, Justin. I hope you don't mean to tell me you don't know the whole town's agog and agape about the chit?"

Over his cards, the Marquis' eyes rested assessingly on his friend's face. "But you are, I believe, evading the issue. You still haven't answered my question. Why specifically now?"

Seeing that Sir Frederick was looking increasingly uncomfortable, the third member of the quartet, a burly individual in his late fifties, broke in. "Lud, Rossington. You must know what he means. That Frenchified relative of yours."

"My aunt?" The Marquis' eyebrows rose fractionally.

"Aye, that's right. The whole town knows she arrived this afternoon."

"Do they so," murmured Saint-Vire. "I congratulate them then, for they know something I do not."

The older man shrugged. He was in no mind to be put off by what he privately thought of as Saint-Vire's vastly affected air. "Stands to reason they're interested. All the old tabbies. Aye, and a good many of the younger ones, too."

"Really." The drawled word was a masterpiece of bored indifference. Anyone not knowing him could have been forgiven for imagining the Marquis had little or no interest in the movements of his relative. Sir Frederick Danvers knew better. He had not missed the slight hardening of that smooth voice, nor the sudden tension in the fingers that gripped the cards.

"I confess to finding myself totally unmoved by the interest of the *ton*," the Marquis added at length.

Lord Bollington, who had been following the conversation with a good deal of secret amusement, gave a short laugh. "Are you so, Saint-Vire?"

His words were ignored.

"Freddy, will you cut?"

Sir Frederick Danvers did as he was bid. Bollington was not a good man to cross, but then neither was Saint-Vire.

A wiser or less meddlesome man might have considered the subject best closed, but Lord Bollington was possessed of a rather malicious turn of mind, and he chose to believe otherwise.

"After all, Saint-Vire, you can't really blame people for being interested, you know."

"No?" The word was accompanied by a lift of the eyebrow that would have instantly quelled lesser men, but that merely served to increase Lord Bollington's amusement.

"Oh come, Saint-Vire. You are a man of the world. You must know what everyone's been saying?"

"Must I, Bollington? How so?"

Lord Bollington shrugged. He was enjoying himself, and he had an audience. Several other gentlemen had put down their cards and wine to listen.

"You claim this chit is your ward."

"Claim, Bollington?" The words were soft with menacing warning, but Lord Bollington appeared not to notice, and merely shrugged his elegant shoulders. "You have to admit it's deuced odd. Who is she? Where has she come from? And who would be foolish enough to make you her guardian? You are hardly the protector of innocence, Saint-Vire ."

There was a shocked, expectant pause.

Many persons might have expressed those thoughts to themselves, or in the privacy of the matrimonial bedchamber to their wives, but few would have dared to say them to the Marquis himself.

"I see. So your concern is all for my ward's welfare, Bollington. You relieve me. I had thought it merely vulgar curiosity."

An ugly flush spread over Lord Bollington's face as a ripple of amusement swept through the club. Saint-Vire had turned the tables on Bollington very neatly.

"Very clever, Saint-Vire," he sneered, "but you have still not answered my questions."

"No?" The Marquis seemed deep in contemplation of his cards. "Perhaps because I do not think them worthy of answer. As you yourself have just remarked, my aunt has arrived from France to chaperone my ward. Exactly how Miss Lawley comes to be my ward is not, I think, a matter for discussion here, Bollington. Neither, I believe, is it a matter for public speculation. Although, of course, if you think otherwise . . ." He left the sentence unfinished, his eyes dropping to the hilt of the sword protruding from the other man's coat. Hastily Sir Frederick intervened.

"So Miss Lawley will be coming out in Society then, Justin?"

The eager manner in which he asked the question owed more to a desire to prevent the outbreak of a quarrel than any real desire to know his friend's intentions, but the spectators, cheated of the challenge that had so recently hung upon the air, waited eagerly for the Marquis' response.

Casually Saint-Vire laid down his cards. "But of course. Why else would I send for Claudine? Had I not intended the girl to take her place in Society, I would have packed her off to Yorkshire."

"So she will make her curtsy?" inquired

one gentleman, abandoning all pretense at interest in his cards.

"Perhaps." The Marquis shrugged. "She has already been received by Louis."

Here was news! The girl had been presented at Versailles.

The Marquis was not unaware of the interest his comment had caused, and Lord Bollington, anxious for revenge, drawled softly,

"But of course. How wise of you Saint-Vire. Put the girl on the marriage mart, by all means. An excellent way to put an end to all the gossip."

"The gossip?" inquired the Marquis delicately.

Lord Bollington, seeing his prey within reach, pounced. "Well, you did leave Paris rather precipitately by all accounts, and naturally one wonders . . ." He too took refuge in delicacy, leaving his sentence interestingly unfinished.

"Does one? But then I was ever a creature of impulse, Bollington." It was plain to the disappointed onlookers that on this occasion at least, the Marquis was not going to satisfy their curiosity.

"Indeed," agreed Lord Bollington affably.

"But it must indeed have been some impulse, Saint-Vire. By all accounts you left Paris in the middle of the night."

The Marquis seemed oblivious to the buzz of speculation. "Dear me, the gossips have been busy, haven't they? But then I am known to be given to the caprice of the moment." Again he glanced significantly at his rapier. "I believe it is your play, Bollington."

It was as if the words held a faint challenge, and for a moment it seemed Lord Bollington would respond. His hand edged toward his side, but then dropped. He picked up his cards.

"As you say, Saint-Vire, it is my play, and I choose Queens!"

A sigh rippled through the club. The entertainment was at an end. Only Sir Frederick remained disturbed, and certain of the more outrageous rumors circulating the town, very much to the forefront of his mind glanced uneasily at his friend.

"I know it matters little to you, Justin, but you must know what people are saying?"

"Must I, Freddy? Pray enlighten me. What are they saying?"

This was the Saint-Vire Sir Frederick most disliked, cold and indifferent, with an edge to his voice that would have sheared through iron.

Heroically he stammered, "They are saying that you have either seduced the chit, or that you intend to."

"Dear me," came the mild retort, "after I have just announced my intention of putting her on the marriage mart?"

Sir Frederick flushed uncomfortably.

A lightening glance encompassed his confusion. "I see. My so respectable peers believe I have sampled the goods myself before putting them up for sale. Is that it, Freddy?"

There was no need to reply. His face betrayed him.

The Marquis' lip curled faintly. "Well, I am

obliged to you for your warning, Freddy, but if you are looking to me to confirm this idle gossip, I'm afraid I must disappoint you. Miss Lawley is nothing more to me than my ward."

Sir Frederick's brow cleared a little.

"Of course not! That is . . . I never thought . . ." He floundered in this fashion for a few seconds before offering apologetically, "It is the ladies, Saint-Vire. You know how it is?"

"All too well, Freddy," agreed the Marquis dryly.

Sir Frederick gave a weak smile. "My sister, Lady Alfriston, gives a rout party or some such thing at the end of next week. I'm sure she would be pleased to send invitations to your aunt and Miss Lawley." He broke off uncomfortably, conscious of the irony in his companion's eyes.

"Trying to protect my ward, Danvers. Most praiseworthy!"

"What? No such thing, I assure you, Saint-Vire."

The Marquis then relented a little. "But there, I know you mean well. I'm sure my aunt will be delighted to accept your sister's invitation, and now, gentlemen, I suggest we leave the subject of my ward, fascinating though you appear to find it, and turn our minds to our cards."

There was no mistaking the faint warning in the cool voice, and the gentlemen settled down once more to devote themselves to the serious business of playing cards.

When the Marquis eventually rose from the tables it was barely gone one o'clock, and pocketing the guineas he had won, he took his leave of his companions.

Lord Bollington watched him go, his face twisted with malice. "I wonder if Saint-Vire is as innocent as he would have us believe? Time was when he thought nothing of sitting over his cards until gone four in the morning."

Sir Frederick shrugged. He too had noticed his friend's strange behavior, but unlike Bollington, had no mind to gossip over it. He wondered idly what Saint-Vire's ward was like, and why exactly they had had to leave Paris. He remembered the way the Marquis had fingered his rapier. Could it have been a duel? And if so, why? He sighed heavily, glad he was not in the shoes of the Marquis of Rossington.

Chapter
11

Georgianna, her spirits raised by the arrival of the Comtesse, spent the whole of the following day listening anxiously for the sound of carriage wheels stopping outside. She had judiciously stationed herself in the main salon so that she might have an uninterrupted view of the square. If the Comtesse saw through these small ploys she was far too kindhearted to remark upon them or upon their ultimate folly.

The morning passed and then the weary, dragging afternoon. Still there was no sign of the Marquis, and Georgianna's spirits steadily sank lower. At last, unable to bear her unhappy face any longer, the Comtesse rang for the carriage.

"You need new slippers," she told Georgianna determinedly, "and a couple of new gowns. Marie has packed all your clothes, of course, but I understand the English ladies are *très chic.*" She said this with an air of patent disbelief. Englishwomen, like their skies, would be gray and dull.

Even if the outing did nothing to improve

Georgianna's spirits, it did at least help to pass the time.

True to his word, Sir Frederick Danvers had lost no time in apprising his sister of the Comtesse's arrival in London, and that good-natured creature had straightway penned a most cordial letter enclosing invitation cards to her rout party.

This invitation was but the first of many.

Not to be outdone, once the news was out that the Comtesse had arrived, other matrons were soon following suit, some of the more daring, or more inquisitive, going so far as to recall that they had surely been introduced to Madame la Comtesse when they had visited Paris. A further inspection of their memories brought to light the triumphant realization that they most certainly had! A morning call was definitely quite in order.

However, they were doomed to disappointment, for upon calling at Rossington House and inquiring after the ladies, they were told politely but firmly that the Comtesse was resting and Miss Lawley was not "at home."

The Comtesse, who was in fact seated in her boudoir and consuming with equal enjoyment a pot of chocolate and the contents of the *Ladies' Journal*, turned her attention to the attendant Georgianna. "*Tiens*, where is Justin? He must know I can do nothing until I have seen him." She gestured to the pile of invitations. "I have accepted Lady Alfriston's—I recall her brother is a great friend of Justin's, but for the others!"

Georgianna, too, was very much aware of

the Marquis' apparent disinclination to visit them.

The Comtesse, however, didn't believe in wasting time over recriminations. Justin would come when he was ready. For now, there was the matter of this ball. Georgianna, they had both decided, would wear the blue.

"We shall give these English something to think about," she declared cheerfully, sublimely ignoring the fact that Georgianna herself was one of that despised race.

The blue gown was unpacked, hung in the closet, and carefully examined to ensure that it had suffered no damage during its transportation. Marie, clucking over Georgianna's ringlets, busied herself bringing them back into some sort of order. The Comtesse decided that perhaps after all a spot of serkis rouge would not come amiss on the night of the ball. It wouldn't do for the child to arrive looking pale and unhappy. Women's eyes were sharp for some things, regardless of their nationality, and Georgianna's defenses were very frail. A glance at that unhappy face, a knowing look in the direction of the Marquis, and *voilà*, the child would be ruined!

Eventually the Marquis did arrive. It was on an afternoon when Georgianna, after a particularly sleepless night, had returned to her bed with aching temples and a quantity of linen pads soaked in Eau de Cologne. The perfume might do much to ease her throbbing temples, but she doubted it could do anything for her equally painful heart.

Saint-Vire found his aunt in the library, huddled over the fire.

"*Tiens*, Justin. This house, 'tis like an ice-house!"

"Aunt, I trust I find you well?"

She ignored the conventional greeting. "I cannot conceive for one moment why you should. Not after what I have been subjected to! Dragged from my bed to find my nephew and his ward gone and all Paris crying that they have eloped! To say nothing of a nauseous journey across the Channel, coupled with a journey in a carriage from which only *le bon Dieu's* mercy enabled me to emerge without a single broken bone."

For a moment the Marquis laughed. The gesture freed him of some of his normal hardness. "Come, Claudine! You know quite well the roads in England are far superior to those in France."

"You haven't asked after Georgianna, Justin," his aunt reminded him quizzically.

He sauntered over to the window. "She is, I trust, quite well?"

"Indeed, although pining a little, I think."

"Pining?" He swung around quickly, gripping the back of a chair. "For Philippe du Plessis, I suppose you mean? *Dieu*, Claudine, what was I to do? Leave her in Paris in the hope that the other *lettre* was not intended for her? Or that somehow du Plessis would be able to save her?"

The Comtesse eyed him thoughtfully. "You could always have encouraged Philippe rather than discouraging him. Perhaps if you had, she would be safely married to him now, and then all this could have been avoided. As it is . . ." She glanced at her nephew and sighed. No need to tell Justin she feared for the child's reputation. He was no fool. He must know the interpretation that would be placed on his actions.

"We have received a good many cards and invitations. So far I have accepted only Lady Alfriston's. I remembered you knew her brother. Perhaps if you could spare the time we might go through the others."

Ignoring the sarcastic overtones to her words, the Marquis sat down. "Give them to me then, Claudine."

There was one lady who remained aloof from the fever of curiosity engendered by the arrival of the Marquis and his ward. Not that she wasn't interested. Far from it! The Countess of Thaxbury had a very keen interest in the Marquis of Rossington, and indeed in everything that touched upon his life, no matter how lightly, and naturally that interest encompassed Miss Georgianna Lawley. Unlike many of her contempories, though, the Countess was in the fortunate position, due in the main to an excellent memory for names, of knowing something at least about Georgianna's antecedents.

The Countess's involvement with the Marquis of Rossington went back a good many years to the time, in fact, when he was newly become the Comte de Saint-Vire, a handsome boy of a little under one and twenty. She herself had been of an age with him. She was the daughter of an excellent and wealthy family, newly come into society from the peace of her father's vast country estates.

The Fourth Marquis of Rossington, always quick when it came to matters touching upon the advancement of his family, had soon discovered that she was in a most fortunate position. She was the sole heiress to her father's vast wealth, and he therefore lost no time in proposing a match between her and his grandson.

The Countess had been over the moon. Justin Ormsby was the catch of the season; already half of London was at his feet—the female half. Barely had she come down from the clouds, having confided the exciting news to the envious ears of no more than a dozen of her "best friends," than the staggering news broke. Justin Ormsby, it seemed, had no intention of falling in with his grandparent's wishes and marrying the heiress. In fact, the young gentleman had been heard to say, somewhat rashly, that he would rather marry a piece of Covent Garden merchandise, they at least provided one with some pleasure. After a quarrel with his grandfather that rocked the sacred precincts of Rossington House, the young gentleman had taken his leave and returned to France, leaving the heiress to face the titters and whispers alone, which even her marriage to the Earl of Thraxton had done little to wipe out. Thraxton was a good enough catch as titles went, but he was a man of five and forty, as opposed to his bride's one and twenty, and he possessed nothing of Justin Ormsby's fabled looks.

She had never forgiven or forgotten the

insult Saint-Vire had dealt her, and the Countess possessed that rare virtue in a woman— patience. It would, she decided, be most interesting to make the acquaintance of Saint-Vire's ward.

London waited breathlessly for Lady Alfriston's rout and their first sight of Miss Georgianna Lawley.

Fortunately for her, Georgianna knew nothing of the gossip that had run through the *ton*, faster than an epidemic of the dreaded smallpox. She was nervous enough as it was while preparing for the party, although it was hard to know whether this was occasioned by the thought of meeting so many new people or a very natural dread of coming face to face with her guardian.

As Marie laced up the back of the blue Chinese gown, Georgianna stared into the mirror. Surely that pensive look had not been in her eyes a few months ago? Or that droop to her lips? Her guardian was an astute man, and it would never do to betray her feelings. This thought was sufficient to achieve a miraculous, although somewhat forced, lightening of her gloom, so that when the Comtesse swept into the room to survey Marie's handiwork she was confronted with a young lady determined to enjoy herself, no matter what the cost.

Eyebrows raised, the Comtesse surveyed the defiant eyes and artificial smile. "That gown is excellent, *petite*. You are ready?" She did not wait for an answer. "Oh, by the way, I nearly forgot. Philippe's letter." She handed her the small package, neither of them making any comment on the fact that Georgianna, knowing she had the letter, had not been concerned enough to ask for it earlier.

The Comtesse tapped Georgianna lightly on the arm. "Read it, *chérie*. Who knows, perhaps it will help to lift your spirits a little. Sometimes it is enough just to know one is loved."

Not if it isn't by the right person, Georgianna's heart cried, but nevertheless she broke the seal and started to read the letter.

"My darling Georgianna,

"By the time you read this, you will be separated from me by the sea. Believe me I could wish it were otherwise. You know, I think, just what you have come to mean to me, and in other circumstances I would have had the honor of requesting you to become my wife. As it is we both know that that cannot be. It is not safe for you to return to Paris, or even to France, and I could never ask you to risk your life by doing so. Believe me, *petite*, I am truly sorry that matters should fall out like this, although I shall always count you among my friends, and hope that you will do the same...."

There was a second page, this time the elegant hand a little disordered, as though the writer was under the influence of some strong emotion.

"Of course, none of this would matter if I did not know in my heart that you belong to another. No need for words or apologies between us, *petite*, or regrets for what might have been. Only this, if you should ever need or want me, I shall come, no matter where you are."

It was signed simply with his name. Slowly Georgianna tore up the second sheet. Philippe would not want careless eyes to see those last few lines. She honored him, even if she could not love him.

"Georgianna, quickly, the carriage!"

She dropped the note onto the table, throwing the torn pieces of paper into the fire.

"Coming. . . ."

Lady Alfriston, who was justly proud of her fine new home in Brook Street, would have been sorely disappointed had she known how little interest her guests were taking of its well-proportioned rooms and fine new furnishings. Later, perhaps, they might recall that the silk wall hangings had been a particularly attractive shade of lemon, or that the china had been the very finest Sèvres and of the very latest design, but for the moment all they were interested in was the arrival of the Comtesse du Farnand and Miss Georgianna Lawley. They were not disappointed. More by accident than anything else, their coach having been held up at the back of the queue and the Comtesse refusing to walk more than half a dozen paces, they were among the last arrivals. Thus it was that the cream of the *ton* assembled in Lady Alfriston's new double drawing room had the unalloyed pleasure of hearing the butler announce firmly,

"The Comtesse du Farnand and Miss Georgianna Lawley."

A dense silence fell over the company.

Dowagers, who should have known better, craned their necks to be the first to get a look at the new arrivals.

Georgianna, unaware of the reason for the silence, paused on the threshold, conscious of a battery of eyes fixed upon her. Nervously she twitched at her gown.

"Claudine, Georgianna."

So smoothly that she was unaware of his presence until he was at their sides, the Marquis detached himself from a group of gentlemen standing by the door.

The Comtesse, seeing Georgianna's vivid blush, felt her heart sink, and Sir Frederick Danvers' eyes widened. "Lud, is that the chit?"

Lord Bollington smiled unpleasantly. "Well, Danvers, do you still believe in his innocence? I vow I don't, and neither do half the people here. A man of Saint-Vire's reputation!"

The Comtesse swept forward on her nephew's arm, and Georgianna followed discreetly behind. Sharp eyes noticed that he bestowed no more than the most formal of greetings on his ward, and that she in turn dropped him a neat curtsy. Nothing could have been more convenable unless, of course, you happened to have been near enough to see the way the chit had blushed, and a good many had.

The Countess of Thraxton has been on the alert from the moment the two ladies had been announced. It could hardly be supposed that a woman of her age and experience could mistake the reasons for Georgianna's all too evident anguish. This was her moment. In a trice she was at the girl's side.

"Miss Lawley?"

Georgianna was uncomfortably aware of being scrutinized by a pair of hard blue eyes. She looked up doubtfully. She had been presented to so many people that she could barely recall their faces, let alone their names.

The Countess addressed her in a kindly tone: "We have not been introduced, I know, but I wanted so much to meet you that I thought we could overlook the formalities."

"Oh?" Georgianna was distinctly wary.

A smile crossed the older woman's face, not quite reaching her eyes, but Georgianna failed to notice.

"Of course you won't remember me." (Indeed, it would have been very strange if she had, for they had never met, but the Countess, a shrewd gambler, was prepared to take the chance.) "How well I recall your dear mother and her kindness to a shy young girl."

Her words had the desired effect.

"You knew my mother?"

The Countess shrugged depreciatingly. "Only a little. I had cousins living near to your parents." (This much was quite true.)

"I chanced to make your mama's acquaintance while I was staying with them. How sad for you to lose her so young."

This ready sympathy made Georgianna forget that she had initially thought the lady's face somewhat on the hard side, and that something about her eyes had made her feel distinctly uncomfortable. She gave her a smile of dazzling radiance.

"I can barely remember her."

The raised eyebrow was indicative of understanding. "No? Perhaps if we were to talk a little. How well I remember that summer. You here just a child at the time, of course, a mere babe in arms."

Happily Georgianna followed her. Only to think of it, this lady knowing her mama!

They reached the sanctuary of a small alcove.

"What I don't understand is how you come to be Rossington's ward?"

"My father arranged it," explained Georgianna.

"Your father? My dear! Your father must have been at least fifteen years older than Saint-Vire. What was he thinking of?"

On the point of blurting out that it had been a mistake, Georgianna hesitated. It was the Countess's cue.

"I trust you will forgive me, child. I wouldn't mention it, but after all, I did know your mama!"

Nervously Georgianna wondered what was coming.

"My poor child!" The Countess was all ready sympathy. "I know you have been chaperoned by Madame la Comtesse, but already London is full of rumors!"

"Rumors?"

Georgianna felt as though the other woman must hear the frightened pounding of her heart!

"Saint-Vire is not the man to have charge of such a very young, and if I might say so, beautiful girl. His reputation alone . . ."

Despite the delicacy of her words, Georgianna's face flamed. "He sees me as a child, nothing more," she protested wildly.

"My dear!" The Countess was all rueful kindness. "A man of Saint-Vire's stamp never! And then, of course, there are your own feelings to consider, aren't there? How long, I wonder, before he discovers them?"

Where her cheeks had been flushed, now they paled. "Bbbbbut . . ."

"Georgianna! Do you think a man of his experience cannot read the signs?"

Anguish seized her. She knew the woman only meant well, but how she longed for her to go away and leave her.

"Of course, Saint-Vire would not make you his mistress—that would be unthinkable. But perhaps a marriage of convenience—it would still the gossiping tongues at least and . . ."

She got no farther. Georgianna was on her feet, swaying slightly, white; her eyes were enormous and dark with suffering.

"My Lady, I . . ."

However, she was not allowed to escape. The Countess had not finished toying with her prey yet. The stupid chit, to go all big-eyed and pale over Saint-Vire. Did she think she was blind? The Countess knew to a nicety what she was feeling. Hadn't she experienced it herself?

"I tell you for your own good, child. Already they are taking bets in the clubs. Saint-Vire will have to marry you if he wishes to protect your reputation. Either that or find you a husband, although . . ." She broke off doubtfully, but Georgianna could supply the words for her. No decent man would now want her.

Georgianna shuddered, unable to bear any more.

"Please, I must have some fresh air."

Blindly, she stumbled past the other woman. The Countess watched her go, a look of extreme satisfaction in her eyes. She had waited a long time to be revenged upon Justin Ormsby, and for once the gods had been more than just.

Georgianna escaped into the garden. Dear God, she could not bear it. She could not marry the Marquis just to save her reputation. She clenched her hands together to prevent them from tembling. No, she could not endure that.

"Georgianna!"

"Oh, Madame."

"Are you all right?"

"A megrim, nothing more."

"Justin is asking for you."

In a listless voice, Georgianna replied, "Is he? I wonder why? I think I should like to return to Rossington House. I don't feel very well."

She could more honestly have said she could not bear to face her guardian, but she did not. She now realized the only course of action left to her.

Chapter
12

"Well, Justin. What are we going to do?"

Claudine stopped pacing the carpet and turned to face her nephew. She had been aroused at the unprecedented hour of ten o'clock that morning by the shrieks of the maid, and the discovery that Georgianna was missing from her room.

Now on the other side of the room her nephew, two crumpled pieces of paper in his hand, stared at her with cold eyes.

"I thought you had some sense, Claudine. You should have given Philippe's letter to me."

"Philippe's letter! You think that is why Georgianna has gone?" She stopped her pacing.

"But, Justin, surely you realize . . ."

"Of course, it's du Plessis' letter. What other reason could there be?"

"What indeed" reflected the Comtesse.

"Besides," continued her irate nephew, "it says so here in this note she left you."

Together they scanned the few lines of hot-pressed notepaper, a few tear stains very much in evidence.

"Forgive me, Madame, but I am so unhappy. I know you will understand."

"What else could make her 'so unhappy' but learning that du Plessis does not care for her as she thought?"

"What else?" agreed the Comtesse *sotto voce*.

"But Justin, think of the scandal when this gets out. Where can she have gone?"

"To answer the latter part of your question first," replied the Marquis grimly, "there is only one place she can have gone. Where else but the one place she can call her own? And as for the scandal, I intend to put an end to that once and for all. This matter of du Plessis has decided me. And now, if you will excuse me, Claudine, I have much to do!"

He halted at the door. "If anyone should inquire for Georgianna, tell them she is abed with a headache."

The Comtesse's eyebrows rose. "And pray how long is this 'headache' supposed to last?"

"She will be back here by tomorrow, I promise you that, Claudine."

The Marquis set out in his carriage in the dank grayness of the cold London morning. The horses made nothing of the journey as the miles flew by under their hooves, but this time he knew what he would find at his journey's end.

The Manor was shrouded in a pale, thin, gray mist curling lovingly around the trees and eddying about his person as he strode into the house. There was no sign of Mrs. Bates. The whole place was still.

He finally found Georgianna in the book room, where she had taken him that first day. This time the curtains were closed, the bright flames of the fire giving the room a warmth and comfort it had not possessed in the cruel spring sunlight.

She was sitting in a chair by the fire, apparently lost in thought. She never even looked up as he swung the door open. The Marquis stood there for a moment and then closed it with a bang.

Georgianna started nervously. "Saint-Vire!" She could hardly believe her eyes. What was the Marquis doing here? She shivered, despite the warmth of the fire, as she saw the grim purpose in his eyes.

"It is thirty miles from London, Georgianna. I am tired, I am hungry, and I am determined. I am not leaving this place without you, so make up your mind to return with me."

The fire crackled and hissed.

She would not look at him, keeping her eyes firmly fixed on the fire, for she knew if she did, she would not be able to prevent herself from running to him and pleading to be taken in his arms.

Soft shadows embraced the room. There might have only been the two of them in the whole world.

"I know you fancy yourself in love with Philippe du Plessis!" His voice was harsh. "It will pass. . . ."

"How do you know? Have you ever been in love?" spoke Georgianna at last.

His mouth tightened, a muscle clenching

in his jaw. "We are not, I think, talking about my feelings, but about yours." The Marquis pushed a hand through his hair, and Georgianna noticed that he seemed unlike himself; he was oddly distraught. "Georgianna, when we return to London our betrothal will be announced."

Fury welled up inside her. He dared to stand there and tell her that, when they both knew he cared nothing, nothing at all for her.

She longed to scream that she would never marry him, but instead she told him formally, "You are very good, my Lord, but I fear you have come on a useless journey. I neither intend to marry you, nor return to London with you in order that you can foist me off on someone else. I must refuse your flattering offer!"

"Refuse!" In two strides he was at her side, wrenching her out of the chair and pulling her around to face him, his eyes glittering. "What folly is this? You know that I . . ."

Her own eyes glittering as much as his, she swept on contemptuously.

"Oh yes, I know you must marry me to protect my reputation," she told him bitterly. "You may be sure I know that. Are we then to perpetrate the Rossington tradition in another loveless marriage?" Her words fell between them, burning like ice.

"And you would have it different?"

"You know I would." There, it was out. No use trying to hide her love any longer. He obviously knew how she felt about him. Well, let him laugh if he wished, let him ridicule and scorn her, but she would not marry him without love.

"I see. But I cannot force Philippe to marry you. You know that, much as I desire your happiness!"

"My happiness!"

Georgianna stared at him with tormented eyes. "When have you cared about that? Right from the start you . . ." She stopped. Tears filled her eyes. "There is no point in dragging all that up now."

"Georgianna!" Her name seemed to come to her out of the distance.

"Go away. Go away," she stormed at him. "Leave me!"

"Very well." His face tightened. "But first, Miss Lawley, you shall have something else to think upon other than Philippe du Plessis, so that you may know what it is like to be kissed by a man who does love you." His arms were round her, his mouth on her own before she could speak, searching, demanding, insistent, and even pleading, in a kiss that would brook no denial, plumbing the very depths of her soul.

"Georgianna!" The word was muffled against her hair. The hands on either side of her face were trembling a little.

"Georgianna! Why can't you love me?"

The words opened the floodgates of her heart. "Justin, I . . ."

"No, say nothing, allow me this at least." Her lips were crushed beneath his, as he kissed her with a slow sweetness that melted her bones and turned her blood to liquid fire, unleashing a thousand intoxicating sensations. Mindlessly she clung to him. Could this really be true? Was she really in his arms? Or was it all a hallucination produced by her own longing for him? If so, she prayed it might last forever.

At last he pushed her from him. "God knows I have fought against my love for you."

"You didn't want to love me?" asked Georgianna.

His face was bitter. "Unrequited love is not a pleasant thing, for the lover or the beloved, as I have cause to know. I had already harmed you enough without that added burden."

"Not even if I told you there was no burden I would rather bear, or that indeed it is one I have been longing for for many a day now?" she asked him softly.

At first he remained so still she thought he had not heard her, and then he was standing staring down into her eyes.

"I hope you are not toying with me, Georgianna, because if you are . . ."

He left the sentence unfinished as she came into his arms, placing her own around his neck, lifting her face trustingly to his.

"I didn't love Philippe, ever. He was a friend, nothing more. Madame knew that; she also knew of my love for you. I thought you hated me, Justin," she told him simply, "and yet I could not help myself. I could not stop loving you."

He, too, knew something of the anguish of an unwanted love. Gently he traced the delicate arch of an eyebrow, his fingers lingering lovingly on the contours of her face.

"I know it in no way excuses my behavior, Georgianna, but I think I knew almost from the start, although I didn't want to admit it. You see, I have always said I would never fall in love, and when I began to suspect I was, and with a girl at least a dozen years my junior, and so innocent it was a sin to even contemplate . . ." He broke off, leaning his face against her hair. "I fought against it. You'll never know how hard. I tried to tell myself I wanted you only as a tool—a means of revenge—but it was no good. I could have killed du Plessis! And all the while my love grew. I wanted you so much it frightened me. For the first time in my life my emotions were out of control. You only had to be in the same room and I . . ." He gestured helplessly. "I was in torment, Georgianna.

She placed her hand on his face. "There is no need."

He captured her hand, pressing an ardent kiss in the palm. "Even now, I cannot believe that you love me."

There was no mistaking, however, the invitation in her eyes.

His kiss swept her to heights she had never imagined, her spirit soaring free as she floated through time and space. His lips at once tender and demanding, pleading and yet masterful. Georgianna remembered the look he had given Anne and that she had envied. It was nothing to the look he turned upon her now.

At last he held her from him. "So. You will have to accept my proposal now."

With a touch of shyness, Georgianna looked

up at him. "I suppose I shall, if only to turn Rossington House into a home."

"A home." One eyebrow rose. "And how, tell me, are you going to achieve that?"

Georgianna blushed and then dimpled a smile. "Our children will make it ring with laughter, and then the ghosts will disappear."

For a moment she thought she had said the wrong thing. Then a tender, almost worshiping look filled his eyes. "Oh my love, only you could have thought of that!"

No need for them to mention his own unhappy childhood, or the other ghosts whose unhappiness tainted the house. All that was needed to be said had been said already in the kiss they had just exchanged. Explanations, plans, they could all come later.

With a touch of his old arrogance he drawled, "Pray allow me to become a husband before I become a father."

He then laughed suddenly as he saw her confusion. "We shall fill Rossington House with our offspring, my love, but all in good time. First I must have my bride."

Blushing, she went into his arms.

The fire crackled again in the grate. Outside it grew dark. There was only the sound of the fire and the softly murmured words of their love.

A month later, a large crowd assembled outside St. George's Church to await the arrival of the bride. All the *ton* were there, and as one dowager murmured to another, "Miss Georgianna Lawley was a very lucky young lady. Rossington, no less! Quite the richest prize on the marriage mart."

As Georgianna entered the church, she heard the quite audible gasps from the people who turned to look at her and no wonder.

In four short weeks the Comtesse had achieved miracles. The wedding, she decreed, would be such that the nobility of England had never seen before. She overruled firmly the Marquis' protests and then Georgianna's for a quiet wedding performed in the chapel at Rossington Park. They were to be married in London, and in style. The gown Georgianna was wearing was a work of art. Tier upon tier of gauzy silk, plain, white, without any additional color, the entire skirt embroidered with diamonds in an intricate pattern that on closer examination revealed the arms of the houses of Saint-Vire and Rossington, cunningly worked and linked together with fine sprays of diamonds so that when she walked they trembled slightly, throwing off shimmering lights. As Lord Bollington remarked to his companion, "Saint-Vire intends to make sure everyone knows the girl is his."

"Wouldn't you?" came the envious response, for lovely though the gown was, it in no way compared with the girl who wore it; nor did the diamonds sparkle more brightly than her eyes when she came back down the aisle on her husband's arm.

The newly married couple paused for a second in the porchway before passing through the waiting gathering. The Marquis bent protectively over his bride, and Georgianna gazed tremulously up at him, in a manner that caused more than one strait-laced dowager to wipe away a surreptitious tear.

Georgianna felt the light brush of her husband's lips against hers, and the now familiar upsurge of joy within her. It was difficult to imagine she had ever felt unloved or unwanted, and her look told him of her feelings.

They smiled ruefully at one another, and then entered the carriage that was to take them north to Rossington Park.

"Well, my Lady?"

"My Lord?" responded Georgianna demurely, as his arms opened wide to enfold her, and her lips melted into sweet surrender beneath his own.